The Four-headed Dragon

"You must leave here immediately!" hissed the scientist, Dubek Krazak. "You are in great danger! I cannot explain now because you haven't a minute to spare." Dr. Krazak then turned and disappeared into the darkness of the corridor. Frank wondered if they were being led into a trap.

"Come on," said Frank. "Keep your light off, Joe. We don't want to be spotted." They went down the stairs as silently as possible.

"I think the door is straight ahead," Joe said. "I've got it."

There was a chilling chuckle behind them, and three flashlights turned on simultaneously. The youths spun around. They could not make out who held the lights, but they could see gun barrels pointing at them.

"Look who we have here," a familiar voice sneered. "Frank and Joe Hardy!"

The Hardy Boys Mystery Stories

Available from MINSTREL Books

69

The

HARDY BOYS®

THE FOUR-
HEADED DRAGON

FRANKLIN W. DIXON

A MINSTREL™ BOOK

PUBLISHED BY POCKET BOOKS

A Minstrel Book published by
POCKET BOOKS, a division of Simon & Schuster, Inc.,
1230 Avenue of the Americas, New York, N.Y. 10020

Copyright © 1981 by Simon & Schuster, Inc.
Cover artwork copyright © 1988 by Paul Bachem

ISBN: 0-671-65797-6

Produced by Mega-Books of New York, Inc.

First Minstrel Books printing February, 1988

10 9 8 7 6 5 4 3 2 1

Contents

THE FOUR-
HEADED DRAGON

1 Surprise Attack

Frank and Joe Hardy were working on a chemical experiment in the laboratory above the Hardy garage when the phone rang. The boys paid no attention. It would be picked up by their mother.

But then Mrs. Hardy's voice came over the intercom. "Frank or Joe, get the phone. It's Chet. He says it's very important!"

Frank reached for the receiver. "He's probably stuck somewhere and wants a lift."

But Chet had no problem this time with his troublesome old jalopy. "Frank, my father found Sam Radley wandering around our farm," he said, his voice tense. "Sam doesn't seem to know where he is. He mumbles, but we can't understand a word."

1

Frank glanced at Joe, who had heard Chet's excited voice. "Tell you what to do, Chet. Call the First Aid Squad, and—"

"Oh, I already did that," Chet interrupted in a hurried tone. "The ambulance is on the way. I also called Sam's apartment three times, but there was no answer. Guess Ethel is out shopping."

"What's Sam doing now?"

"My father and Iola managed to get him into a chair and my mother made him a cup of coffee. But he won't drink it. He just stares into space with his hands on his knees. I tell you, it's scary. Frank, I have to go. Here comes the ambulance. They sure are quick."

"We're going to drive to the hospital right now!" Frank said before Chet hung up.

Then he turned to his brother. Joe was already putting away the equipment they had been using for their experiment. Frank buzzed the main house on the intercom.

"Yes?" Aunt Gertrude replied.

"Joe and I are rushing to the hospital," Frank told her. "Sam Radley's been hurt. Tell Mom, will you?"

"I will," Aunt Gertrude said and cut off the conversation immediately. She never asked questions during an emergency.

2

In a minute, the boys were in their yellow sports sedan and moving down Elm Street.

"I wish Dad were here," Joe said.

"We'll notify him as soon as we can," Frank told his brother.

Sam Radley and his wife, Ethel, were good friends of the Hardy family. Sam and Mr. Hardy, who had once been an ace detective on the New York police force before he went into private practice, had been working together for years.

Frank thought of that as he turned into Main Street. A siren shrieked behind them. He looked back. "Here comes the ambulance!"

Quickly, he pulled the car over to the curb and stopped. The ambulance tore by on the way to the hospital.

As Frank was moving out into the mainstream of traffic again, someone honked the horn frantically behind them. He slammed on the brakes as a large black sedan swerved to miss them and almost hit an automobile coming from the opposite direction. The black car did not slow down, but continued after the ambulance.

Joe let out his breath. "That was close!"

"That driver never even looked back!" Frank complained. "Too bad there's no patrol car around. A cop could have nabbed him for speeding and

3

going over a double line. Did you get a look at the driver?"

Joe shook his head. "Not a peek. I tried to catch the license plate number, but the car was going too fast."

Frank moved ahead cautiously. "My theory is that guys like that get caught eventually. I just hope it happens before he kills someone because of his recklessness!"

They arrived at the hospital a few minutes later, and met Dr. Kelly in the lobby. "How's Sam Radley?" Frank asked.

"Oh, is that who's down in emergency?" the physician asked.

The boys nodded.

"I'm on my way there now. You two sit in the lobby. I'll get back to you as soon as I've examined the patient."

Twenty minutes later, the doctor reappeared and sat down. "It's an odd case," he said. "Sam seems to be in shock, and yet it's not quite that, either. He doesn't have any wounds and, as far as I can discover, no broken bones. I'm going to have X-rays taken, though, to be sure."

"Can you make an educated guess as to what it might be, Doctor?" Frank asked.

Dr. Kelly knitted his brow. "This is no diagnosis, you understand, but his condition is somewhat

4

like concussion. I served three years overseas with the army, and I've treated soldiers who were too near a shell when it exploded. They were not hit, but they received the shock of the blast. Sam reacts like those soldiers—mumbling, incoherent, nearly motionless—the thousand-yard stare."

"Thousand-yard stare?" Joe asked.

"He doesn't seem to see what's directly in front of him, but is looking at something far away," the doctor explained. "Very common for soldiers who have been in combat for many days. Just why Sam should be affected that way is a mystery to me. Has anyone contacted Sam's wife?"

"Chet Morton tried to phone her, but she's not in," Frank replied.

"Well, I suggest that you contact Mrs. Radley as soon as you can. Her husband is in no great danger, but she should be here. Perhaps, if he sees her, he'll snap out of his condition."

Dr. Kelly left, and Frank and Joe went to a phone booth to call Ethel Radley. After the phone had rung ten times, Frank hung up.

"Why don't we go over to the apartment?" he suggested. "Maybe a neighbor has an idea where she went."

"Good thinking," Joe agreed.

On the way, Frank snapped his fingers. "I should have thought of it before! Do you remember the automatic answering machine the Radleys bought last month?"

"Sure," Joe said. "Sam made us call them three times to make certain it was working."

"Then why didn't it answer?"

"Maybe Ethel forgot to turn it on when she went out."

"That's not like her," Frank said. "She's so careful about everything."

"Could be the machine is on the blink," Joe suggested.

"It's possible, but I have a feeling something's wrong." Frank smoothly pulled up in front of the Radley's apartment building and the boys rushed into the lobby.

"Did you see Mrs. Radley go out this afternoon?" Frank asked the doorman, who was sweeping the floor.

"No, I didn't," the man replied. "I only came on at four o'clock, though. She hasn't gone out since then."

"Thanks." Joe jabbed the elevator button. It seemed forever until the doors opened on the lobby floor. Frank punched the button marked "17" and up they went.

The Radley apartment, 17E, was at the end of the hall. The boys walked rapidly toward it.

"Look, the door's slightly open," Joe cried. He marched in, followed by Frank.

It was dark in the living room. "Where's the light switch?" Frank asked tensely.

"A little to your right, I think," his brother said.

However, Frank did not have time to turn on the lights. There was the sound of heavy footsteps from the other side of the room, then three bodies slammed into the Hardys.

Frank and Joe had been trained to react quickly when ambushed. Joe seized the right arm of the nearest attacker and pulled the man to the floor on top of him. Then he twisted in a way that would have made his high school wrestling coach proud of him. Now he was on top.

Frank was pinned to the wall by two other assailants. He kicked sharply and felt his shoe make contact with an ankle. One man screamed and released his grip. Frank turned his attention to the other fellow, swinging a skillful right cross to the stranger's head.

But the battle came to an abrupt end. Joe couldn't hold down the stocky man beneath him. The thug heaved the boy off to one side. Then the intruder, whose ankle had been kicked, growled, "Let's get out of here!"

The three rushed for the door. They retreated so

7

quickly that neither Frank nor Joe were able to stop them.

Frank managed to reach the door just as the trio was disappearing into the elevator. He saw only their backs, but he noted with satisfaction that one was limping badly.

"I'm going after them!" he called out to Joe and took up the pursuit. If he were lucky, the elevator would stop several times on the way to the lobby. He raced to the fire exit stairs and flew down as fast as he could.

Maybe someone with a lot of luggage will hold up the elevator, Frank thought. Perhaps someone will move a piece of furniture—

But his wish did not come true. When he arrived in the lobby, panting and out of breath, the elevator doors stood open, and there was no sign of the three men. The doorman was nowhere in sight, either.

Frank rushed out to the street, but the men had disappeared without a trace. Disappointed, the boy went up to the Radley apartment again. Everything was quiet as he entered, and the light was still off. A chill went down Frank's spine. Had something happened to his brother?

2 Night Scare

Frank switched on the light. "Joe, where are you?" he cried in alarm.

"Over here," came a muffled voice from behind the couch. Joe slowly emerged, looking disgusted.

"Are you hurt?" Frank asked.

"No." Joe rubbed his neck. "But that guy flipped me as if I were a pillow, even though I'm taller than he is and outweigh him by a few pounds. Anyway, I landed on my head and blacked out for a minute." He surveyed the room. "What a mess!"

Pictures had been ripped off the walls, chairs and the couch had been overturned, drawers had been pulled out and their contents heaped on the floor.

9

Even the carpet had been taken up and tossed in a corner.

The kitchen, bathroom, and bedroom were in the same condition. The most serious damage was in the spare room Sam used as an office. The cards that the detective had carefully compiled for many years on hundreds of criminals had been taken out of the file box and now littered the room from wall to wall. The automatic answering machine had been smashed.

"Well, whatever those thugs were looking for they didn't find," Frank observed. "Otherwise, they'd have been gone by the time we arrived."

Just then they heard a thumping from the office closet. Frank leaped to the door and flung it open. Ethel Radley was lying on the floor, her hands and ankles tied and her mouth taped. She had been kicking her heels against the door.

They freed her from her bonds and carried her to the living room couch. Joe brought her a glass of water. She sat quietly for a few moments, her eyes closed.

At last, she looked at the two anxious youths and said, "I never thought I would get out of that closet."

"Can you tell us what happened," Joe asked, "or would you like to rest some more?"

"No, no." She shook her head to clear it. "I'm all

right. I want those people caught before they hurt someone else. I went out to shop and returned a little after one o'clock. Two of them were already here, going through everything. They tied me and put me in the closet. All afternoon I listened to them moving around, smashing things. I tried to hear what they were talking about, but caught very little of their conversation. They were discussing a dragon, that much I could hear."

Joe and Frank stared at her in amazement. "A dragon?" Joe asked.

"Yes."

"Do you remember anything else? What they looked like? If they referred to each other by names?"

Ethel Radley thought carefully. "It all happened so quickly that I had only a slight impression of their appearance. One was tall with dark hair and another was fairly short. It was this last one who tied me up. He was very strong."

"Sounds like my sparring partner," Joe said wryly, remembering how he had been tossed. "But there were three of them. You didn't see the third man?"

"No, he came in later." She knitted her brow. "Wait a minute. The phone range. They answered it and probably talked to the third man."

"How did they do that?" Frank asked, perplexed.

11

"We called twice and they didn't pick it up."

"It must have been a code," Ethel suggested. "It rang three times and then stopped. Then it rang again after a minute and one of the men said, 'That must be Carl.'"

"Carl," Joe repeated thoughtfully.

"Anyway, one of them picked up the receiver and listened. Then he said. 'Well, follow the ambulance and find out where they're taking him.' Then he hung up."

Frank and Joe looked at each other. "That must have been the black car that almost hit us," Joe said.

"You know something about this?" Ethel asked.

Frank explained what had happened, then said gently, "Do you feel better now?"

"Oh, yes."

"I'm afraid I have some more bad news for you. Sam was found wandering around the Morton farm. He didn't seem to know where he was. The ambulance took him to Bayport Hospital."

"What!" Ethel's hands flew to her face. "Poor Sam! How is he now?"

"Physically he appears to be all right," Frank replied. "But he's disoriented. He still doesn't know where he is. That's why we've been trying to get in touch with you and why we came here."

"I have to go to him!" Ethel cried.

The boys helped her to her feet. "We'll drive

you," Frank said and took her arm. Although she was still shaky, she managed to walk out to the car.

Sam's condition had not changed. Ethel sat by his bed, anxiously watching her husband's face. "You two can run along now," she said with a wan smile. "I'll stay with him."

"You ought to eat something after what you've been through," Frank said. "We'll have a meal sent in to you."

"Thank you," she said.

"If Sam says something that you can understand, would you please write it down?" Joe handed her a pencil and a page from his notebook. "Don't worry if it makes little sense. You never can tell when a clue will pop up."

A twinkle returned to Ethel's soft gray eyes. "You sound just like Sam."

"And our father," Frank remarked. "Which reminds me that we have to get in touch with him. Come on, Joe."

The youths stopped at the hospital coffee shop to order a hamburger and a soft drink for Ethel. Then they started home.

As they drove down Main Street, Frank said, "I wonder what Sam was working on. If we knew that, we'd know how to proceed."

"Maybe Dad has an idea."

Fenton Hardy, an internationally known detective, was often asked by the federal government to help on difficult cases. At the moment, he was in Alaska working with the FBI.

When the boys arrived home, Aunt Gertrude called to them from the kitchen, "Dinner will be ready in ten minutes!"

"We have to phone Dad first," Frank told her as he and Joe headed for the study.

"Your mother is talking to him right now," Aunt Gertrude informed them.

"Here they are," Mrs. Hardy said into the phone as her sons entered. "Don't hang up. They'll tell you what's been going on." She looked at the youths curiously. "As a matter of fact, I would like to know, too. I've been waiting all afternoon for a phone call from you."

"Sorry, Mom," Frank apologized as he took the receiver. "Everything happened so quickly, we didn't have a chance."

He related the events of the past few hours to his father.

"That's just terrible," Mr. Hardy said in a troubled voice. "I don't know what Sam was working on. It must have come up very recently. I spoke to him three days ago and he mentioned only a few routine things. Of course, he might have been trying to contact me since, but I've been away from the office. I had to go underground and even the

14

FBI didn't know where I was." Mr. Hardy spoke calmly about what must have been a dangerous assignment.

"I'm flying home immediately," he continued, concern in his voice. "Fortunately, my work in Alaska has been completed. The case is not solved, though. We'll have to pick up clues somewhere else. Good-bye, Frank, I'll see you tomorrow."

"Good-bye, Dad. Have a good flight."

Frank had just put down the receiver when Aunt Gertrude stuck her head into the study. "If you don't come right now, the food will be cold," she announced.

The two women asked questions all during the meal and Frank and Joe answered between bites of delicious lamb stew.

"I'm glad your father is returning," said Mrs. Hardy. "It seems as if he's been away a month."

"Not to change the subject," Aunt Gertrude remarked, which meant she was going to do exactly that, "but did you hear about the hurricane that is approaching North Carolina? I hope it won't veer and hit Bayport."

Mrs. Hardy smiled. "There are lots of hurricanes at this time of year, and most of them amount to nothing. Anyway, North Carolina is a long way from here, Gertrude."

"That's what everyone said several years ago,"

Miss Hardy said tartly. "And look at the hurricane we had then."

Frank chuckled. "I don't think you should worry about something that might never happen."

"Oh, you're right," Aunt Gertrude replied. "But I believe in the Boy Scouts' motto: 'Be prepared.' I'm going to lay in a supply of canned food and condensed milk early tomorrow morning just in case we lose electricity again."

After dinner, the boys phoned Sam's hospital room. Ethel Radley said that, although the detective was resting more easily, there was little overall change in his condition. She had not been able to make out any words from her husband's incoherent ramblings. Dr. Kelly had been kind enough to have a cot set up for her and meals sent in. She would let them know immediately if Sam awakened.

"But do me a favor," she added. "I haven't called the police about the break-in yet. Will you do it for me?"

"Sure," Frank promised. He reported the incident to the sergeant on duty, then he and Joe went out to the garage laboratory and completed their chemistry experiment. It was their way of relaxing.

Later, they sat in the kitchen, drinking cocoa and going over the mysterious events of the afternoon. They came up with several theories, but rejected each one after careful consideration. At last, unable to find a suitable answer to Sam's delirium or the invasion of the Radley apartment, they went to bed.

They were awakened three hours later when Aunt Gertrude shook them. Joe snapped on the table lamp between the two beds, but their aunt put her finger to her lips to command silence and switched off the light.

"I've been listening in bed to my radio earphones in case there was any new information about the hurricane," she whispered. "When I took the earphones off, I heard noises downstairs."

The boys stared at her. "I don't hear anything," Joe stated. He and Frank knew how vivid their favorite aunt's imagination could be, especially coupled with the possibility of a hurricane. The sounds, they suspected, might be a figment of her imagination.

"How could anyone get in?" Frank asked. "We have a burglar alarm system. No one could—"

"I know what I heard!" Aunt Gertrude insisted in her usual tart manner. "Now, do you want me to go look or will you?"

The boys groaned inwardly, but slid out of their beds and went to the landing. There they became wide awake in an instant. From below came very faint but unmistakable sounds in the study. They retreated to their bedroom.

"Please phone the police, Aunt Gertrude," Frank

whispered as he and Joe pulled on pants and shirts in the dark. "Then go to Mom's room, tell her what's happening, and lock the door. We're going downstairs."

Aunt Gertrude gripped their shoulders. "On second thought, maybe you'd better wait for the police!"

"The burglars may get away if we do," Joe pointed out.

"Then be very careful. Don't take any unnecessary chances!" Aunt Gertrude slipped out of the room noiselessly.

Frank and Joe slowly crept down the carpeted stairs. Frank stopped at the right side of the room their father was temporarily using as a study, since his study upstairs was in the process of being redecorated. Joe took his post at the left.

"Well, there's nothing about the four-headed dragon here," came a low, rough voice from within. "Let's try the other rooms."

The boys instantly remembered the reference to dragons by the burglars of the Radley apartment, but their thoughts were interrupted by another voice.

"I don't like this, not with those kids upstairs."

"Oh, you're always scared, Carl," a third man sneered. "That's all they are, kids."

"Strong kids," Carl reminded them.

18

There was a soft snort. "I handled one of them this afternoon all right."

Joe clenched his fist, aware that he was listening to the man who had tossed him in the Radley apartment. We'll see who wins the second round, he said to himself.

"We can't stay here all night yakking," said the first man, who was obviously the leader. "Come on, let's get moving."

The Hardys tensed as the door opened. Then, as the masked intruders emerged, Frank snapped on the hallway light and he and Joe jumped the strangers.

For the second time in a few hours, they were battling the same crooks, but now they had the advantage of surprise. They were fighting evenly, too, because one of the men broke loose from the melee and ran out the front door.

Joe once again found himself struggling with the smallest of the gang. He pinned the thug against the wall. The man's mask fell off to reveal a face crossed with scars.

Then Joe heard a thud. Out of the corner of his eye, he saw Frank on the floor, his assailant standing over him with a blackjack. The man raised the weapon for another devastating blow. With a shout, Joe released the small man and hurled himself at Frank's opponent.

His fist caught the crook's chin and the man staggered backwards. The thug recovered quickly, though. He held the blackjack high, menacing Joe, who was standing over Frank's inert form!

3 Warning in the Woods

But the blackjack never fell. "Let's get out of here, Slicer," the man called to his unmasked companion.

The other needed no further persuasion. Together, the two backed toward the now open front door as Joe glared at them, his fists ready.

"We'll meet again, sonny," the small man growled just before the burglars disappeared into the night.

As soon as they had left, Joe turned his attention to his brother. To his surprise, Frank was still conscious, although he was very groggy.

"Go . . . after . . . them, Joe. Don't . . . worry about . . . me."

"Mom, Aunt Gertrude!" Joe shouted. The two

21

women appeared at the head of the stairs. "Frank's been hurt! Take care of him, will you? I'm going after the burglars!"

"No!" his mother cried, but Joe was already out the door. He saw the thugs getting into a black car across the street. Joe sprinted for the garage, opened the door, and jumped on his motorcycle. One pump of his foot and the bike roared.

Down the driveway the youth drove and into Elm Street in pursuit. The black sedan went a few blocks and turned into Main Street.

Maybe I'll see a patrol car, Joe said to himself. The small city was quiet. They passed stores, houses, and gas stations where not a light showed— but there was no sign of the police.

Joe stayed two blocks behind the sedan, trusting that the criminals would not spot him. Apparently, the three men felt safe and did not look back. After passing through the business district, they turned onto a country road, going well below the speed limit.

The driver probably doesn't want to draw any attention to himself by going fast, Joe thought.

They drove on for a couple more miles. Just after they passed the entrance to the Morton farm, Joe's motorcycle began to sputter and lose speed. Finally, the engine quit and he drifted to a stop.

Joe knew very well the reason for the engine's

failure and scolded himself. He had been low on gasoline and had delayed filling the tank!

He pushed the cycle into the bushes. When he was sure it could not be seen from the road, he started jogging home. As he passed the Morton farm again, he thought of turning in to borrow Chet's car. But it would not be fair to wake the family.

Fifty minutes later, he turned into the Hardy property. Lights were on downstairs and a patrol car was parked in the driveway.

Aunt Gertrude, Mrs. Hardy, Frank, and Police Chief Collig, who had been a friend of the family for many years, were in the study. They looked up as he entered.

"Well, what happened?" Frank asked.

Joe shrugged his shoulders and told them the story of the empty gas tank. "So I wasn't able to accomplish anything," he concluded. Then he turned to his brother. "How are you?" he inquired.

"He should be in bed," Mrs. Hardy put in, "but he insisted on waiting for you."

"The police took me to the hospital," said Frank, "and I was checked out, X-rays and all. No concussion or anything like that. I must admit, though," he went on with a wry smile, "that I have a whopper of a headache."

"Sergeant Moore informed me about the break-in of the Radley's apartment and Sam's condition," Chief Collig spoke up. "I'm sure these crooks are professionals and won't be easy to track down. You have the most sophisticated burglar alarm system I've ever seen, yet they managed to dismantle it without your knowledge. It takes an electronics genius to do that."

"You're right," Frank said. "And both times the intruders mentioned something about dragons. Do you have any idea what this could refer to?"

The chief shook his head. "None. I've never heard of anything like this."

"Did you see Sam, Frank?" Joe asked anxiously.

Frank shook his head. "Ethel was sleeping on the cot and I didn't want to disturb her. A nurse told me, though, that his condition has not changed."

Chief Collig rose. "Nothing more to be done here for the present," he said. "Just one question, Joe. Did you manage to get the license plate number of the black car?"

"I wasn't able to pull up close enough," Joe replied. "I was afraid they might see me if I narrowed the gap."

Chief Collig nodded. "That was wise. But we have very little to go on, except that one of the thugs, Slicer, is small and has a scarred face.

24

Another is called Carl. And something about dragons. I don't mind saying I'm glad your father's returning today. It's not that I don't admire your talents, boys, but I suspect that this particular gang is very dangerous!"

Frank and Joe had always been early risers, but this morning, exhausted by the events of the previous night, they slept until nine. They would have remained in bed even later if they were not awakened by a bustle from downstairs.

Coming into the hall, they were met by Aunt Gertrude. "You'll have to get your own breakfast," she informed them, "and please don't get underfoot today. Mr. Rogers is on his way over to start laying new carpeting, and your mother and I are getting the house ready for the work."

"We won't be in the way," Joe promised. "We'll be going to get my motorcycle."

When the boys had finished eating and were on the way out, Aunt Gertrude burst into the kitchen followed by the carpet dealer, Mr. Rogers, and a stranger.

"We also want carpeting in here," she declared. She cast a sharp eye on her nephews. "Leaving?" she asked.

"Yes," Frank said. "Hello, Mr. Rogers."

"Hello there, Frank, Joe. I'd like you to meet my new assistant, Ben Ebler."

The large, broad-shouldered man with the genial, smiling face held out his hand. "It's a pleasure meeting you," he said. "I read about your exploits in the California newspapers. You certainly have acquired quite a reputation for yourselves."

"You're from California?" Joe asked.

"I've lived out there for ten years, but originally I'm from Boston. I like California, but my relatives are here in the East, so I thought I would return to my roots for a while."

"Is Curt away on vacation, Mr. Rogers?" Frank inquired. Curt Gutman had been Rogers's assistant and carpet layer for many years.

"Just came back," Mr. Rogers replied grumpily. "He would be on this job, but when I arrived at my store this morning, I found a note from him. Said he had to go to Philadelphia immediately to visit a dying aunt. Humpf, I didn't even know he had an aunt. Never mentioned her. Anyhow, it was lucky that Ben came in with letters of recommendation from some of the best rug dealers on the West Coast. I hired him on the spot."

"I'll be around here for a few days," Ben explained, "but I'll do my best not to get in the way of anything you're doing."

"Well," Aunt Gertrude exclaimed, "nothing will be done if we stand here gabbing all morning! You boys said you were on your way out."

Frank winked at Joe. "We're already gone, Aunt Gertrude."

They rode off in their yellow sports car. When they were approaching the Morton farm, Joe suddenly yelled, "Stop, Frank! Quick!"

"What's the matter?" Frank pulled over to the side of the road and jammed on the brakes.

Joe didn't hear him. He had his head turned and was staring after a gray car that had just passed them going to Bayport. "I think that was him!"

"Who?"

Joe turned back, scowling. "Remember the guy that knocked me out at Sam's—Slicer? I'm pretty sure he was driving that car!"

"Then let's go after him!" Frank suggested excitedly.

"There's no chance to catch him," Joe said gloomily. "He was going fast, well over the speed limit. Anyway, maybe it wasn't him. I only had a quick glance at the driver."

"Well, if it was Slicer, they have more than one car!"

Joe nodded, and the boys got out. They easily found the spot where Joe had left his motorcycle. He was struggling to pull it out of the bushes when a cold voice remarked, "You are trespassing on private property!"

A young man, not much older than the Hardys, appeared from the woods. Joe smiled at him. "I thought this was part of the Morton farm."

"It is not! It is the Sayers' estate!"

Joe started to explain that he had run out of gas in the early morning and was forced to hide the bike in the bushes, but the other interrupted him rudely. "Please, no excuses. Do not set foot on the Sayers' property again or it will mean trouble for you."

With that dire warning, the young man crept back into the foliage. Joe looked at Frank, puzzled. "Now what do you think that was all about?"

"Your guess is as good as mine. He's a foreigner, that much is for sure. I couldn't make out the accent, though. Could you?"

Joe shook his head. "Eastern European would be my guess."

"Another thing puzzles me," Frank said. "The Sayers' property has been deserted for years, except for Emile Grabb, the caretaker!"

4 A Dangerous Scheme

Joe filled the gas tank and started the motorcycle. He noted with satisfaction its steady roar. Apparently, the bike had not been affected by its night out.

"Let's stop in at the Mortons," suggested Frank. "I had only a few words with Chet yesterday. Maybe I missed something about Sam in the rush or Chet forgot to mention an important clue."

"Good idea," said Joe.

Frank drove up the dirt road leading to the farmhouse, followed by Joe on his motorcycle. Chet's pretty, dark-haired sister, Iola, came out of the kitchen door, wiping her hands on an apron. "Hi, Frank, Joe. Chet's out on the tractor, but he ought to be here in a few minutes. Come on in. I've just made a cake and you can sample it."

29

"Glad to," Joe said, getting off his bike. "Only don't you think Chet would be a better critic? He's had a lot more practice at cake testing than I have."

The pixie-faced girl's eyes twinkled as she laughed. "Oh, his appraisal isn't worth too much. He'll eat *anything*."

She turned serious. "How is Sam?"

Joe was about to tell her when Chet came in. "Wow, chocolate cake!" he exclaimed. "But you've already given these guys most of it."

"Most of it!" his sister protested. "Why, they only had two small pieces."

Chet winked at his two best friends. "Looks like most of it to me," he said, cutting himself a large slice. "Say, how's Sam?"

The boys gave Chet and Iola their meager information concerning Sam's condition and then filled them in on the events since yesterday.

Chet whistled when they were finished. "This is terrible! My father figured that maybe a large branch had fallen from a tree and hit Sam on the head, giving him a concussion. But Dr. Kelly doesn't think so, huh?"

"No head injury at all," said Joe.

"Hello there, Hardys," boomed a voice, as Mr. Morton entered the room, followed by Mrs. Morton. "Glad to see you. How's Sam?"

Once again, the boys repeated their tale. The farmer shook his head. "Well, I hope he pulls out of whatever ails him."

"Say, Dad, did you hear anything about new people moving in next door at the Sayers' estate?" Iola asked.

"Not a word. Is it true? I've been waiting for years to have new neighbors. Always good to have friends nearby to visit and chat."

"I don't think they'll be too friendly, judging by the person we met," Joe said, and went on to describe the threatening young stranger in the woods.

Mr. Morton rubbed his chin. "He doesn't sound very hospitable. But then, they have a right to keep people off the property, I guess."

"By the way, Dad, I saw tracks of the wild dogs near the sheep pen," Chet stated, helping himself to another piece of Iola's cake.

"That high wire fence kept them out, I guess," Mr. Morton surmised, "but they're getting more daring than ever."

"I thought you liked dogs, Mr. Morton," Joe said.

"I do, but I can't say I'm particularly fond of the wild pack that formed about four years ago. Two or three dogs started to live in the woods. I figured they escaped from cruel owners. They weren't too much trouble at first, but now the pack has grown to

31

about fifteen. They've been after our sheep and chickens. Poor mutts, they're really in misery. Most of them are diseased. I've been asking the town government to round them up, but they keep dragging their heels. I'm afraid sooner or later those dogs are going to attack human beings!"

"That's an awful thought!" Frank glanced at his watch. "Mrs. Morton, would you mind if I called home?"

"Not at all. You know where the phone is. Help yourself."

Frank and Joe went into the hall where the telephone was. Frank dialed and their mother answered.

"Come back right away and pick me up," she said. "Jack Wayne just called over the radio. Your father's plane is half an hour away from landing at Bayport."

"We're on our way, Mom," Frank replied.

After saying good-bye to the Mortons, the boys left. They pulled into the Hardy driveway fifteen minutes later.

They ran into the house where their mother was ready and waiting for them.

"Wait a minute," Frank said before they went out the front door. "I want to get my tape recorder. Perhaps we can tape Sam's mumblings." He took the stairs two at a time, almost tripping over Ben

Ebler, who was laying carpet in the upstairs hall. "Sorry," he said.

"Think nothing of it," the man replied.

A few moments later, Frank drove the car out into Elm Street.

"That was a good idea to bring the recorder," Joe complimented his brother. "I hope it works."

When they were walking through the parking lot at the air terminal, Mrs. Hardy pointed upward and said, "That's what I call good timing."

The boys followed her gaze and saw *Skyhappy Sal*, Jack Wayne's silver-winged plane, gliding down. Jack piloted Mr. Hardy whenever necessary. By the time Mrs. Hardy and the boys had walked through the terminal, he was taxiing to the building.

Fenton Hardy was the first off. After kissing his wife, he turned to the boys. "Has there been any change in Sam's condition?"

"Not as far as we know," Joe replied, "but we haven't checked today."

"Then we'd better get to the hospital as fast as possible." The detective turned to his pilot, who had just emerged from the plane. "Jack, we'll run you home so you can get a well-deserved rest."

"Thanks, Fenton, but you go on ahead. I have to leave instructions about servicing the plane first," Jack Wayne said.

"Are you tired?" Mrs. Hardy asked her husband as the automobile moved out of the parking lot.

He leaned back and smiled. "I caught some sleep on the way. Jack certainly knows how to fly a plane smoothly."

"It's like riding on air, right, Dad?" Joe commented.

Everyone laughed, then Mrs. Hardy asked her husband if he would be able to stay home for a while.

He sighed. "I'm not sure when I will be called in again. The Alaska phase is completed and the FBI has to pick up the leads I uncovered elsewhere."

"Can you talk about the case, Dad?" Frank asked.

"Yes, but I have to warn you that you're not to breathe a word about it. The plot is so diabolical that it's almost unbelievable. If the story appears in the newspapers, people might panic."

"That serious?" Mrs. Hardy inquired.

"I would say that the possible destruction of the Alaskan pipeline is indeed serious," her husband replied soberly.

"The Alaskan pipeline!" gasped the boys together.

"None other. A few weeks ago, U.S. Intelligence services picked up strange rumors that Burl Bantler, an American criminal, has been contacting unfriendly foreign governments, claiming that he can destroy the Alaskan pipeline with a secret weapon.

"Apparently, one country—we don't know which —bought the deal, for recently Bantler has been seen in Alaska. That much I uncovered."

"Do you think he's still there?" Mrs. Hardy questioned anxiously.

"No. It seems I just missed him in Nome by a few hours. Now he has left the state, but the word is that he'll return with the weapon."

"He must be stopped!" Mrs. Hardy exclaimed.

Her husband nodded. "He bragged that he doesn't mean wiping out just a section of the pipeline, but the entire thing. I don't have to tell you what effect that would have on our country."

"A good deal of our oil supply would disappear," Frank commented, "until the pipeline is rebuilt, which would take years."

"Right," Fenton Hardy said grimly.

"How do you know that Bantler isn't faking, Dad?" Joe asked. "Maybe this weapon doesn't even exist."

"That's a possibility," the detective admitted, "especially considering that Bantler, besides his other criminal activities, has been a con man. But I doubt that he would try such a scam on a foreign government.

"Second," Mr. Hardy went on, "Bantler has

35

never before been involved in espionage. I don't believe that he'd get into it if he didn't have a real weapon. Third, why would he go to Alaska after contacting these foreign governments? If the entire thing was a confidence game, he would have gone underground after collecting his money. Or, what's more likely, he wouldn't even have collected if he hadn't had some convincing proof of what he's able to deliver."

The famous sleuth's face was set in rocklike determination. "This man has to be stopped. If not, our country may be in very bad trouble!"

5 Sabotage at the Airport

"It's unfortunate that Sam is injured at this particular time," Fenton Hardy said as he, Mrs. Hardy, and the boys entered Bayport Hospital. "Not only is he a close friend, but he once arrested Bantler and would be able to recognize him. I've never seen the man and don't have much of an idea what he looks like."

"Don't you have a description?" Frank asked, puzzled.

"All I really know is that he's a large man," Mr. Hardy replied. "You see, Bantler is a master of disguises. And Sam, as you know, is a master of seeing through disguises. Probably the best in the country."

Ethel Radley looked worried and tired as the boys and their parents entered the hospital room. Dark rings lined her eyes. "He just doesn't change," she said, when asked about Sam's condition. "He's calmer, but he's still delirious."

Fenton sat by the bed and talked to Sam for a few minutes, but there was no response from the ill man, except a continual, nonsensical mumbling. Finally, the detective rose, sighing. "Let's go and confer with Dr. Kelly."

"Joe and I'd like to stay here, Dad," Frank said, "and tape what Sam is saying."

Mr. Hardy nodded and left the room with his wife and Ethel Radley.

Frank checked the recorder to see if it was in working order before placing the machine on Sam's pillow. Then he and Joe sat back in their chairs. However, Sam was now quiet.

After fifteen minutes had passed, the silence was broken by the shrill sound of the telephone. The boys jumped, startled by the ring.

Joe picked up the receiver.

"Hardys?" asked a rough voice on the other end.

"Who is this?" Joe questioned sharply.

"You're Joe, right? Just wanted to warn you to lay off this case. Don't meddle any more. What you're doing is dangerous!"

38

Joe recognized the voice. "We don't pay any attention to threats, Slicer."

There was a half-gasp and then a buzz as the line went dead. Joe hung up slowly, shaking his head. "I made a mistake. I should never have mentioned his name. But I did hear his buddy call him Slicer last night."

"He may not have realized that his name had been spoken during the fight," said Frank, "or he may have thought that you hadn't heard it."

Joe nodded glumly. "Now he knows we know his name."

A few moments later, Fenton Hardy came back into the hospital room. "Dr. Kelly is convinced Sam will snap out of it sooner or later," he said, and looked with pity at the man in the bed. "I only hope it's sooner. Did you record anything?"

"The tape just came to an end," Frank said. "I don't know if anything's on it because the phone rang. We'll study it at home."

He told his father about Slicer's call when the telephone rang again. The three of them stared at it.

"Do you think Slicer's calling back?" Joe asked.

"Only one way to find out," the detective declared and picked up the receiver. "Fenton Hardy here. Oh, it's you, John. How did you track me down here? Gertrude told you? Good. What's up? What? Great! That may be the break we've been waiting for! Chicago? Sure, I'll meet you there. Good-bye."

The boys looked at their father expectantly when he hung up, but he held up his hand to prevent questions and dialed again. "Hello, Jack. Sorry to bother you so soon, but the FBI just phoned. Yes, I'm afraid we're off again. Perhaps I should get another pilot for this trip? No? Okay, I appreciate that. I'd rather fly with you than anyone else. I'm off to the airport right now and I'll meet you there. No, no change in Sam. I'll see you."

Once again, he put down the phone. "You two bring the car over to the front entrance. I'll meet you there in five minutes after I talk to your mother."

The boys were full of questions, but they had been trained to act quickly and obey orders during an emergency. They turned on their heels without saying a word and left the room.

Frank had just pulled up in front of the hospital when Fenton Hardy came running out. He jumped into the back seat and they drove to Main Street.

"Go to our house and wait while I pick up some clean shirts," the detective said. "Then we'll continue on to the airport. I'm off to Chicago. That was FBI Agent John Mortini on the phone. An associate of Burl Bantler's has been picked up. He saw Bantler only a month ago, but he isn't talking yet."

40

"Do we return to the hospital to get Mom after you take off?" Joe asked.

"No, she wants to stay with Ethel this afternoon. Doctor Kelly will drive her home when he finishes his shift at five o'clock."

As they pulled up to the Hardy residence on Elm Street, a car parked at the curb moved away. Aunt Gertrude was pruning roses in the front yard. Fenton Hardy dashed over to her. "I have no time to talk, Gertrude. The boys will fill you in on what's going on." With that, he continued on into the house.

Frank quickly told his aunt about the search for Burl Bantler and his father's trip to Chicago.

She sighed. "He's always on the go. I know what he's doing is very important, but he simply must get a little relaxation sometime. He hasn't had a vacation in years!"

"Who was that in the car pulling away?" Joe asked. "The driver certainly seemed in a hurry."

"Ben Ebler," she said. "He received a phone call just before you arrived. He turned white as a sheet and ran off after shouting to me he had to leave because of an emergency, but would be back tomorrow."

"Poor man," Joe said. "I hope there's no trouble."

Fenton Hardy ran out of the house, shirts tucked under his arm. He gave Aunt Gertrude a peck of a kiss on her forehead and jumped into the car.

She cast an appraising eye on him as Frank started the engine. "You look pale and tired. All this gallivanting around is not doing your health a speck of good. I imagine you haven't had any lunch yet."

"Don't worry, I promise to have a big steak when I arrive in Chicago," he said.

"With plenty of green vegetables," she called as the car backed out onto Elm Street.

"She treats you just like she treats us, Dad," said Joe with an innocent air.

"I'll worry when she doesn't," the detective said, waving good-bye to his older sister. "Now there are some things I want you to do for me," he explained, placing the clean shirts in his suitcase. "Before I left Alaska, I requested the FBI to ask all the police chiefs in the country to send me any data they might have on Burl Bantler—anything, no matter how insignificant. This information will come to our home since I'm never sure where I'll be from one minute to the next. It'll be your job to receive the data and summarize it so that you can give it to me in a nutshell when I phone."

"When will that be, Dad?" Frank asked.

"I can't tell you exactly. I'll try to make it daily and perhaps more often, but I don't know at what time."

They drove directly to the hangar instead of the

42

air terminal's parking lot. As they got out, they saw a red-faced Jack Wayne gesturing excitedly at Sy Kramer, the head mechanic. The boys had never seen the pilot so angry.

"You know, Sy, that you and I and your own mechanics are the only people allowed to touch this plane, and no one else!" Jack thundered.

"What seems to be the problem?" Mr. Hardy inquired.

"Some guy waltzed in here wearing a white coverall and claimed I sent him to service the *Skyhappy Sal.* He showed a phony note reportedly from me, confirming the order," Jack shouted. He turned back to Kramer. "Sy, didn't it occur to you to phone me and see if it was okay to let this guy work on the plane?"

"Well, he seemed all right," the chief mechanic replied with an embarrassed shrug.

"Seemed all right!" the pilot exploded. "Seemed all—"

"I'm sure Sy believed he was doing the correct thing," Mr. Hardy said in a conciliatory tone, even though tension showed in his face. "Anyway, it's too late now. What should be done next, Jack?"

"I'm sorry to delay the flight, but you'll have to admit this is highly suspicious. I want to go over the plane from nose to tail."

"You're right," Mr. Hardy agreed.

As the pilot walked into the hangar, the detective turned to Kramer. "Sy, what do you remember about this fake mechanic?"

"Well, he had a rough voice. He was small, about five foot five, I would say, but strong, bulging with muscles. His face has a number of crisscrossed scars."

The boys looked at each other. "Slicer!" Frank exclaimed. "You remember, Dad, the thug we told you about?"

"I remember," Mr. Hardy said, his expression grim. "First he searches our house for something, then he tries to sabotage my plane. I wonder why?"

While Jack and Sy worked on the aircraft, Mr. Hardy and his sons went into the terminal to report the incident to the police. When they returned to the hangar a half hour later, Jack walked toward them, his overalls greasy. "Lucky Sy mentioned this guy," he said. "I found a small leak in the fuel line. It was so tiny that I was fortunate to discover it."

"What would have happened if you hadn't?" Mr. Hardy asked.

"We would have run out of fuel in about an hour or a little after. That would have been in the Great Lakes area. If there'd been an airfield nearby, I might have been able to glide in, but in all probability we would have crashed into the water!"

44

6 Vicious Dogs

Mr. Hardy's face was grim but calm. "Did you find anything else wrong, Jack?"

"The plane's okay now," the pilot replied. "I'll stake my life on it." He grinned. "Come to think of it, that's what I'm doing, right?"

The detective smiled. "If you say the *Skyhappy Sal* is in good shape, then it must be. Let's go!"

The boys watched the plane taxi down to one end of the runway and then roar along the concrete until it lifted off into the cloudless sky, heading west.

"Dad sure asked the million dollar question," commented Frank as they walked back to the car.

"What's that?" Joe asked.

"Why Slicer sabotaged his plane. Does what's

45

happening have something to do with the Bantler case?"

"It's possible," Joe admitted.

On the way home, they saw a familiar figure on Main Street, kicking the tires of an old, battered jalopy. They pulled up to the curb and Joe called, "Chet, what are you doing?"

Chet gave the tire a final, powerful kick and looked up at them. "This dumb old thing is giving me trouble again."

The brothers laughed. "The car isn't human, Chet," Frank said. "It doesn't know what it's doing."

"Or not doing," Joe added, smiling.

"Well, it sure acts like it does," Chet grumbled. "I tell you, this jalopy's got a grudge against me. Lucky for me I met a stranger who has more sympathy than you two." He waved toward the upturned hood, which came down with a sudden slam.

"I'm afraid, son, that you have carburetor trouble," Ben Ebler said. "Oh—hi, there, Frank and Joe. You know this unfortunate young man?"

"We have watched him eat anything in sight since he was in kindergarten," Joe explained. "With luck, we'll be watching him doing that for the rest of our lives."

"I'm still growing," Chet defended himself.

46

"In all directions," Frank observed, glancing significantly at his friend's stomach. "Coach won't like that when you go out for football."

"Oh, I'll be in shape by the first game," Chet replied airily. "Say, how about taking me to Gordon's Garage?"

"At your service," said Joe. He opened the trunk and took out a towline, then Frank pulled their sports sedan in front of Chet's old jalopy.

"Can we drop you anywhere?" Frank asked Ben as Chet and Joe attached the line.

"No, thanks," Ben replied. "Haven't got far to go."

"Aunt Gertrude was concerned that you had to leave so suddenly this afternoon," Frank went on. "Nothing serious, I hope."

"Family problems out of town," the man explained. "But everything is cleared up now. Tell your aunt I'll be at your house bright and early tomorrow morning." He waved good-bye and sauntered down the street.

"Nice guy," Joe said as he hopped back into the car, while Chet got behind the wheel of his disabled jalopy. "Helping a total stranger is what I call real kindness."

At the garage, Mr. Gordon looked grim after he had examined the engine. "That Ebler fellow diagnosed it just right, Chet. Needs a new carburetor. I don't have any in stock. It'll take at least a week to get one."

After Mr. Gordon had told him the price, Chet looked unhappy. "I've just lost my appetite," he said to Frank. "Could you drive me home?"

"Your wish is our command," Frank replied. "But Joe will be your chauffeur. I'm going home to find out if anything's on the tape we have on Sam."

The boys climbed into the sports sedan, and Joe tried to comfort his friend. "Maybe you can make some extra money cutting lawns," he suggested.

Chet sighed. "You realize how many lawns I have to cut to pay for a new carburetor? It'll take me all summer!"

Frank laughed. "That'll keep you out of mischief!"

Chet gave him a withering glance as Joe pulled up in front of the Hardy home to let Frank out. Then the two drove on to the Morton farm. Just as Joe was about to turn into the lane leading to the farmhouse, they heard cries for help ahead.

"Someone's in trouble!" Joe exclaimed, passing the Morton entrance. They went over a small bridge and reached the spot where they thought the cries had come from, but could see no one.

"Maybe somebody's playing a joke," Chet guessed.

"We'd better check," Joe said, his head hanging

out of the car. He switched off the engine, then Chet, too, heard the calls.

"It's coming from the woods," Joe declared. "Let's go!"

He dashed in among the trees, followed closely by Chet, who was fast despite his size. They had gone a hundred yards when they came into a small clearing. A young woman had her back to a tree and was staring horrified at a pack of wild dogs. The animals, saliva dripping from their mouths, were growling as they slowly advanced on her.

"Don't shout any more!" Joe called to her. He walked a few steps toward the dogs and then began to jump and yell.

The animals turned. They were malnourished and covered with sores. Some were so thin that their ribs were pushing against their skins. Joe knew they were to be pitied, but all he felt was fear. He had hoped that they would flee when he and Chet burst upon the scene, but they apparently saw them as other and better victims. One dirty white-and-brown mastiff, obviously the leader, pushed through the pack and advanced on the Hardy youth while Chet backed off in fear.

Joe thought quickly. "I'll draw them off!" he yelled at Chet. "Get her in the car and go for help!" Then he ran deeper into the woods, pursued by the pack that now started to howl, excited by the hunt.

Chet reacted quickly. He rushed to the terrified young woman and seized her wrist. "Come on!" he shouted in her ear to shock her out of the horror that made her motionless. Together they fled toward the road.

When they reached the car, Chet ran around to the driver's side. However, his feet became tangled in a vine and he fell to the ground. He struggled to rise, but by the time he had settled himself behind the wheel, he discovered that the girl had disappeared. He looked wildly around, but there was no sign of her. Quickly he backed the car up to the entrance of his home, then shifted into drive and shot up the lane.

He jumped out of the car and burst into the living room where Iola and his father sat reading the newspaper. "Joe's being chased by the wild dogs out in the woods!" Chet called out.

Mr. Morton sprang up without a word and began to unlock the gun cabinet to get his shotgun. Iola ran for her jacket, while Chet dialed the phone. Fortunately, Frank answered right away at the Hardy house. Chet tersely told him of Joe's plight and Frank promised to come immediately. Chet hung up just as Iola returned and Mr. Morton finished loading the gun.

The trio ran out to the Hardy's car. Chet drove

back to the spot where the boys had run into the woods. He was surprised to see the young woman and a man her age running toward them.

"My friend, Tonio," she said breathlessly, waving at her companion. "He knows the way of the woods."

"That's why you left?" Chet asked as he, his sister, and father emerged from the car.

She nodded. "He will be of great help."

"I can track," Tonio confirmed. "I was brought up in forest land." Chet noted that he, too, spoke with a foreign accent.

"We need all the help we can get," said Mr. Morton. "Is this where you went into the woods, Chet?"

"That's right. You can see where we trampled through the bushes."

"Then lead the way."

Chet plunged into the underbrush, the others on his heels. Soon they came to the clearing where he and Joe had found the mysterious young woman facing the vicious animals. But now there was no trace of either the younger Hardy or the dogs!

"What do we do?" asked Chet helplessly. "I can't remember in what direction Joe ran."

"Wait!" Tonio ordered, holding up his hand.

They all held their breath for a full minute. "I don't hear anything but birds," Iola said at last.

51

"Nor do I," said Tonio. "I thought we might hear the baying of the pack. I shall have to find the trail."

He walked around the clearing for a few minutes, his eyes intently on the ground. Twice he moved out of the glen in a specific direction, but each time he returned, shaking his head. "I thought that was it, but I was wrong."

The stillness was broken by a faint whir from the road that became louder and louder until they recognized it as the sound of a motorcycle. Then the vehicle's engine stopped and they heard Frank call, "Chet!"

"In here, Frank," returned his friend. In a few moments, Frank burst into the clearing. Chet quickly told him that the young woman and Tonio had come to help find Joe. Frank recognized Tonio as the unfriendly stranger that had accosted him and Joe that very morning, but he said nothing.

"I have it!" Tonio exclaimed. "Come!" They followed him into the foliage.

A thick mist had settled in the forest and it was growing dark quickly.

"I hope he can see the trail," Chet whispered to Frank, his eyes on Tonio, who was now bending low while steadily moving ahead.

After he had left the glen, Joe had managed to keep ahead of the pack by running as fast as he could. He was getting tired, though, and knew he could not maintain the pace. The dogs were gaining on him. Already the leader of the pack was snapping at his heels.

About a mile from the clearing, Joe came to a rapidly running stream that divided the Morton property from the Sayers' estate. He was faced with the decision of whether to jump in and try to swim to safety or not. Too much of his strength had ebbed away, so he grabbed the low-hanging branch of a tree and swung himself up. The leader of the pack made a desperate leap, but his teeth snapped on empty air an inch from Joe's leg.

Joe paused a moment to recover his breath, then slowly climbed two branches higher. Beneath, the animals howled for a few minutes. Then they sat and quieted, waiting for their prey to return to the ground.

"Not today, fellows," Joe said to them, "if I can help it."

The trees were closely bunched along the bank of the stream. Perhaps, he told himself, I can get away by moving from tree to tree. Gingerly, he reached out to the next one and grabbed a branch. Over he swung.

His pursuers silently moved until they were beneath him again. He went to the next tree and then the next, but they always followed.

He traveled safely through ten trees, but the eleventh was a mistake, which he realized immediately. It had been dead for a long time and needed only a violent storm to bring it down.

The branch he landed on cracked beneath his weight. He almost followed it down, but at the last second he was able to seize another. It, too, creaked dangerously. Afraid that it might not hold him much longer, Joe removed his shoes, tied the laces together, and hung them around his neck.

The beasts below growled in anticipation. Was the stream deep enough? He didn't have time to wonder. As the branch crumbled, he jumped, landing feet first in the water.

Luckily, it was at least eight feet deep. When Joe's toes struck bottom, he pushed himself up. He emerged just in time to hear a crash behind him. He looked back and saw to his horror that the dead tree had fallen into the stream. The swift current was rushing it toward him. He flung up a hand to escape it, but managed only to partly divert it. The torn end of the rotten trunk struck him a glancing blow and he slipped into unconsciousness!

7 Narrow Escape

Fortunately, Joe was unconscious only for a moment. The cold water revived him and he floated down the stream as the wild dogs ran along the bank. Their mouths were open and their sharp teeth gleamed.

Joe tried to swim to the other bank, but gave up after a few strokes. He was too exhausted from running and from the blow on his head.

I'd better just float for a while until something turns up, he said to himself. Unfortunately, what turned up was a slowing of the current. The water had been too swift for the dogs to swim in, but now the leader saw its chance. It dove in and paddled after the Hardy boy. Joe saw to his horror that the beast was thirty yards away and gaining rapidly.

Then came a stroke of luck Joe had been hoping for. Before him loomed a small island. It was fortunate that the tide was out; otherwise, it would have rushed up the small river from Barmet Bay, completely submerging the little mound of mud and twigs.

Wearily, Joe pulled himself onto the land and turned around. It was only a matter of seconds before the dog reached the island. It came out of the water, its scraggly fur dripping, and advanced on Joe as the pack on shore howled with anticipation.

Joe frantically looked around for a weapon—a rock, a branch, anything, but there was nothing but slippery mud!

Meanwhile, Tonio led the way through the darkening woods, the rest of the party following closely. Suddenly, they heard the howling of the dogs ahead of them. "They're not far away!" Tonio called out.

"I just hope we're in time," Chet muttered, panting. He shivered, not from the cold air, but from thinking about the diseased and hungry wild animals. Frank, by his side, said nothing. His mouth was set in a grim line as they quickened their pace.

Joe took his shoes from around his neck as the pack leader came nearer and nearer. He put his right hand around the knot that tied them together, then swung the shoes above his head.

The stalking beast stopped, startled for a moment. A low and steady growl arose from its throat. Its hind legs went down and its entire body tensed for action.

Then the dog sprang through the air in a mighty leap. Joe was prepared for the charge and timed his blow just right. The heavy shoes caught the animal on the jaw and it fell to one side, landing on its back, yelping.

Joe turned to face the beast, his shoes again swinging for the next blow. But he never had to deliver it. The dog scrambled to its feet and quickly jumped back into the water.

Just then, the rescue party came into view. Mr. Morton sized up the situation in a split second, lifted his shotgun, and let off a blast above the heads of the dogs. Away they ran, followed by the mastiff, whose tail was between its legs.

"Am I glad to see you!" Joe yelled.

"Can you get over here," Frank asked, "or do you need help?"

Joe looked at the span of water. "Are you kidding? Sure, I can." He put his shoes around his neck again and plunged into the wide stream. Frank eyed his brother anxiously. It was evident by his slow strokes that the younger Hardy's energy had been depleted by the efforts of the past hour. Happily, though, Joe did not have to swim all the way. His feet touched bottom and he was able to walk the last twenty feet.

When he arrived, his friends and Frank pounded him on his back and pumped his hand.

"Better get up to the house," Mr. Morton said, "and put on some dry clothes before you come down with pneumonia." He looked around the clearing in which they were standing. "You know, something's funny here, though. Something I can't put my finger on." He frowned thoughtfully, then cried out, "I have it! There was an old shed here. My father built it a long time ago to store wood he cut, and for axes and saws. I've never used it, but I saw it last winter. Now it's gone!"

"I think we should leave," Tonio suggested. "The dogs might return."

"I doubt it. They're scared to death. They may be capable of attacking a single person or helpless animals, but not a whole group." As he spoke, Mr. Morton walked around the clearing, his eyes glued to the ground. "What's this pile of dust?"

He leaned down and picked up a handful. "This is where the shed was. Did you ever see anything like this?"

Everyone except Tonio, who held back, gathered

around the farmer and stared at the dust. "It's as if a billion termites had a banquet," he said, and shook his head.

"I think your friend is shivering," Tonio said, and pointed at Joe.

"You're right." Mr. Morton glanced at the Hardy boy, who was, indeed, shaking. "We can talk about this mystery later," the farmer said, and took off his heavy jacket. He put it over Joe's shoulders. "Come along."

Soon the party arrived at the farm. Mrs. Morton was standing in the door. "I was getting worried. I came back from shopping and no one was here. You didn't even leave a note," she said.

"Didn't have any time." Mr. Morton told her what had happened.

"Those dogs!" she exclaimed. "I just hope the township government will listen to you this time and round them up. Chet, you better take Joe up to your room."

While Joe and Chet were gone, Iola and Mrs. Morton busied themselves in the kitchen. Mr. Morton, Frank, and the two strangers sat in the living room. Conversation was attempted by both Frank and Mr. Morton, but Tonio's attitude cast a pall over the scene. He sat buried in a chair, hands in pockets, and staring at the ceiling. The young

59

woman threw him imploring looks to improve his manners, but he ignored her.

When Joe came downstairs, however, the atmosphere was lightened by the sight of the younger Hardy wearing his friend's clothes.

Frank laughed. "You look like a circus clown."

Joe looked at himself in the mirror and, seeing the baggy trousers and oversized wool shirt, grinned sheepishly. "I guess I do."

"Those clothes look all right," Chet protested.

"On you they do," his smiling father replied.

"They're warm and dry, anyhow," Chet said defensively.

Just then Mrs. Morton and Iola bustled in, carrying trays of sandwiches. Everyone took something, even Tonio, who mumbled his thanks.

"I would like to thank you for rescuing me from those horrible dogs," said the mysterious young woman to Joe and Chet. "You risked your lives to save mine."

"All in a day's work," Chet said airily. Then, glancing at Joe, he added shamefacedly, "Of course, Joe did the most."

"Are you from around here, dear?" Mrs. Morton asked the young woman.

The stranger's smile lit up her dark eyes. "No, both Tonio and I are from thousands of miles away. Permit me to explain. My name is Maquala Krazak

60

and my friend is Tonio Mossesky. At the moment we, my father, and my uncle are your next-door neighbors."

"You are staying at the old Abby Sayer mansion?" Mrs. Morton asked, her eyes widening.

"For the time being," Maquala said with a touch of sadness in her voice. "It seems we are always on the move, but I shall be sorry to leave Bayport, for it is a very nice place. We lead what might seem exciting lives to many people; however, it is far from pleasant to be always running from agents who are following us, even in this country, escaping from prison, and—"

"Maquala, they don't care to hear about all that," Tonio broke in. "Anyway, it is getting late and your father—"

"To the contrary, we are very interested," said Mrs. Morton. "Please go on, my dear."

Tonio receded into his sulk as the Mortons and the Hardys leaned forward to hear the story.

8 Telephone Trap

"We are Huculs," began Maquala.

"You are what?" asked Iola.

Maquala laughed. "I know you're puzzled. Not many people outside of Eastern Europe have heard of us. The Huculs are the people who live in the Carpathian Mountains. Some of us live in Poland, some in Czechoslovakia, and others in Romania, but we are one people with our own culture.

"My father, Dubek Krazak, is a great scientist. That's not only my opinion, but scientists all over the world say so. It that not true, Tonio?"

Her friend gave a short nod, but continued staring at the ceiling.

"All the countries behind the Iron Curtain want

him to work for them. Believe me, they have tried many times. They have begged him, they have offered him a soft life, and they have threatened him. But he has always refused to serve them. He hates oppressors and loves the democracy he has never enjoyed until he came to this country."

"How long ago was that?" Iola asked.

"Only a few months back," Maquala replied. "When Father was young, he fought against the Nazis. After the war, he fought other oppressors. He has been a leader of the Resistance and, oh, what a price he has paid! What a price we all have paid!

"Neither I nor Tonio have ever known a permanent home. Often we have been awakened in the middle of the night to flee minutes before the secret police arrived.

"Sometimes, we were not quick enough and my father and my uncle, Alessandro, were arrested and taken off to prison. My mother and Tonio's mother and father died in prison. But my father and my uncle always escaped."

The girl sighed, then continued. "A few months ago, it became obvious that there was no place in Eastern Europe we could stay. My father had become too well known. Also, he is crippled as a result of the tortures he has endured, and his health is poor. Thus, it was decided that we should come to the United States. We rented the Sayer house, but we might have to move on soon. My father has been told that secret agents are searching for us even here. Meanwhile, he is working on an invention that he hopes—"

Tonio stood up abruptly. "Maquala, I must insist that we leave. Your father will be very worried."

He held her coat and she rose reluctantly. "I suppose you're right," she said. "Again, I wish to thank you, Joe, for what you did. You saved my life. You were very, very brave."

Tonio's hostile eyes flashed at her praise of the younger Hardy. Joe noticed the Hucul's annoyance and said, "If it hadn't been for Tonio, I would have been the one who might have been killed."

"Yes," joined in Frank, "I don't see how you could track through those dark woods, Tonio. You're a great woodsman."

The young man was not pacified by the compliments. He mumbled something no one could hear and began to hustle Maquala towards the door.

"Please come again," Mrs. Morton invited. "After all, we're next-door neighbors."

"I don't think that's possible," replied Tonio stiffly. "We are very busy."

But Maquala smiled. "Thank you. I will try. It becomes very lonely sometimes."

"Well, I guess we ought to be going, too," said

Frank. "We're expecting a phone call from Dad."

"What will I wear home?" said Joe in dismay. "I mean, my clothes are still wet and—"

"Oh, you can wear mine and return them to me later," said Chet generously. He examined Joe carefully, from the baggy trousers to the tentlike shirt. "No matter what anyone says, you really look great."

"Oh, go soak your head," Joe returned good-naturedly. He playfully tapped his friend on the arm. "Say, I never saw you run so fast in my life as you did in the woods. You ought to go out for the sprints next spring."

"I have talents I haven't even discovered yet," Chet agreed, puffing himself up a little.

When Frank and Joe walked in the front door of the Hardy house, they found Aunt Gertrude carrying a large basket of papers. "These are telegrams," she said grumpily, "from police all over the country. They've been arriving every five minutes all afternoon. Something about a man called Bantler." Then she stared at Joe in amazement. "Where did you get those clothes? It's too early for Halloween and, anyhow, I thought you had outgrown trick-or-treating."

"Tell you later," Joe said hastily, heading toward the stairs.

Frank took the telegrams into the study where

Mrs. Hardy looked up from the phone. "Ethel Radley just called. Sam is better," she said happily. "He's resting more easily and seems to be coming around."

"Has he awakened at all?" said Frank, depositing the telegrams on his father's desk.

"No, he's still semiconscious, but Dr. Kelly is very much encouraged and believes he'll wake soon."

Aunt Gertrude came in the room with an announcement. "That hurricane I told you about is not going to hit North Carolina after all," she said. "The radio says it has bypassed that state and now is headed north. I just hope it doesn't hit us." She looked around triumphantly. "All of you thought I was foolish to worry about that storm, didn't you? Well, it appears my intuition was right!"

She was so proud that the boys were almost sure their aunt would be disappointed if the hurricane didn't come. But they kept these thoughts to themselves.

"What's your afternoon been like?" Mrs. Hardy asked her sons. "Did your father get off all right?"

"The takeoff was beautiful," said Frank with a meaningful glance at Joe, "and the weather between here and Chicago was reported to be just fine. I'm sure he arrived on time."

"Oh, he did," said Aunt Gertrude. "He phoned

from Chicago while your mother was at the hospital. He had a good trip."

Frank avoided mentioning the fake plane mechanic and the puncture in the gas line. No use worrying his aunt and his mother, he decided. Joe nodded in silent agreement.

"But seeing Fenton off wasn't all you did this afternoon," Aunt Gertrude commented, looking at Joe. "You came home in those funny clothes and your hair was wet, as though you had been swimming."

"Not by choice," Joe said, and launched into an account of the day's events.

The two women listened intently. Mrs. Hardy shook her head when he finished. "I wouldn't want to live in the Sayer mansion. It can't be very comfortable. It hasn't been occupied for years. Emile Grabb has been doing his best to keep it in good condition, I'm sure, but he lives in a small cottage on the grounds. Anyway, what can one person do to maintain such a huge house?"

"All I know about the place is that it is old and spooky and on a high bluff," Joe said. "Who was Abby Sayer, anyway?"

Aunt Gertrude's eyes became misty. "Hers is a sad story, a tragedy, in a way. She was the only child of a wealthy clothes manufacturer. When she was very young, she witnessed a terrible thing—her

67

father's factory being burned to the ground. It was only a short way from her house and she saw all the corpses being carried out."

"Oh, no!" Joe exclaimed.

"She never forgot it," Aunt Gertrude went on. "What was worse was that the people of the city blamed her father, although it was proved it was not his fault. Hardly anyone would speak to the family and she had a lonely and unhappy childhood. It did something to her mind. She somehow had the idea that she was being haunted by the ghosts of the workers who had died in the fire."

"That's terrible," Frank said sympathetically.

Aunt Gertrude nodded. "Anyway, after her parents died, she moved to Bayport and built the mansion. I've never been in it, but I hear that it was the strangest house that was ever constructed."

"It *is* a strange house," said Mrs. Hardy. "My friend Joan MacLeod, whose father was a butler for Abby Sayer, told me a great deal about life there."

"What was it like?" Joe asked curiously.

"Abby Sayer never stopped adding on to the mansion. She had carpenters working all the time. You see, she believed that the ghosts of the dead workers had tracked her down and that she had to make them comfortable or else they would do something horrible to her. By the time she died, the mansion had over three hundred rooms."

"Three hundred rooms!" Joe whistled. "That's a hotel!"

His mother nodded. "Miss Sayer designed the place herself and she certainly dreamed up some very strange architecture, such as passages that led to blank walls, trapdoors, and stairways so small that you have to crawl up them."

"Crazy," Frank commented.

"Wait till you hear what happened each night! Abby had a steeple constructed with a huge clock on top. It only tolled once in 24 hours and that was at midnight. Then the servants would bring the most delicious food to the banquet hall on golden plates. She would greet her twelve ghostly guests as she sat down at the head of the table. Then the servants would leave, shutting the door behind them."

"Twelve invisible guests and herself made thirteen," observed Frank.

Aunt Gertrude chuckled. "The right number for such a ghoulish affair. I'll say this for Abby Sayer, though: she may have been a bit touched in her head, but she had a heart of gold. She provided the money to construct the Bayport Youth Clubhouse. And just look at the way she befriended Emile Grabb. He was an orphan, friendless and alone, as she had been, but she took him under her wing and made him her chauffeur and general aide. He worshipped the ground she walked on. Still worships her, I suppose, for he stayed on after she died to take care of the gloomy place."

"How long ago did she die?" Joe asked.

"I can't remember exactly," Aunt Gertrude said, "but it seems like it was ten years ago or thereabouts. No one has lived in the house since. The story is that her lawyers never could figure what to do with the old place. Now, at last, they've rented it."

Just then the telephone rang. "I'll get it," Frank replied and went to pick up the receiver.

"I'd like to speak to either Frank or Joe Hardy," said a pleasant male voice.

"This is Frank."

"Oh, good. I'm Ted O'Neil and I'm a nurse at the hospital. Dr. Kelly asked me to phone you. Sam Radley is wide awake and very anxious to talk with you and your brother. Could you come over at once?"

"We'll be right there," Frank replied.

"Good," said O'Neil. "Oh, by the way, he was told how you recorded him. He'd like to hear that. Can you bring the tape?"

"Sure will. Say, can I talk to Sam now?"

"Dr. Kelly does not want Mr. Radley to overexert himself," the male nurse said a bit nervously. "As a matter of fact, you'll be able to see him for only a few minutes."

"I understand. Good-bye."

70

Excitedly, Frank related the good news to the others.

"That's great!" exclaimed Joe, rising. "I'll get my coat."

"No!" Mrs. Hardy said sternly. "You're in no condition to go out. You go straight to bed and get a good night's sleep. Otherwise, you may end up in the hospital with Sam."

Joe knew better than to argue with his mother when her mind was made up. Also, he recognized the wisdom of her words.

"All right," he replied, "but, Frank, you wake me when you get home and let me know what Sam said."

Frank drove down Elm Street. The worry of the last two days was partly lifted from his mind. Sam was getting better and might be able to tell him exactly what had happened on the Morton farm. Mr. Hardy was getting a lot of helpful information on the elusive Bantler that might stop the criminal before he could damage the Alaska pipeline, and the mystery of the strange young man who had ordered them off the Sayer property had been cleared up.

Frank paid little attention to a car coming up behind him. When it started to pass, he thought angrily that the driver was being reckless by speeding and crossing a double line.

Then the car cut Frank off and forced him to the curb. Two masked men leaped out and opened the door of his car before he could close the windows and lock himself in.

They pounced on the boy and, even though he tried to fight them off as best he could, they pinned him behind the wheel and pommeled him mercilessly.

"The tape!" one of them hissed. "Give us the tape!"

9 *A Sad Story*

One man reached into Frank's coat pocket and pulled out the cassette. "Got it!" he cried triumphantly. "Let's go!"

"First, let's give him a lesson he'll never forget," his companion growled. "We'll teach him not to meddle in something that's none of his business."

They continued to hit Frank who was pinned on the front seat of the car. Suddenly, the blows ceased.

"Let him alone!" came a familiar voice.

The Hardy youth looked up and saw Ben Ebler pushing the assailants away from his yellow sports car.

Suddenly, the smaller of the two crooks pulled

out a gun. "Get back!" he ordered Ben Ebler.

The carpet layer slowly put up his hands. "You rats!" he snarled.

"I ought to shoot you," the gunman said.

"Come on," the other urged. "The cops may come by. We've got what we came for."

The gunman hesitated and then backed to his car. "I don't know who you are," he said to Ebler, "but we'll meet again!"

"You'd better hope not," Frank's rescuer advised.

The thugs' automobile roared down the street as Ben Ebler bent over Frank. "You all right?"

Frank shook his head to clear it. "I think so. No broken bones or anything. They didn't hit that hard."

Ebler helped him out of the car. Steadying himself with difficulty, Frank said, "Did you get the license plate of that car?"

Ebler snapped his fingers. "I should have thought of it. Sorry, Frank."

"Don't worry about it," Frank said. "No reason you should think of it. I'm just thankful that you arrived."

"It was lucky at that," Ebler agreed. "I had eaten a heavy dinner and thought I would take a walk to work it off. I saw them cut you off, but I was a block away and couldn't get here any faster. Why do you think they jumped you?"

"I don't know," Frank said casually. "Probably a couple of muggers." Fenton Hardy had taught his sons never to divulge a secret to anyone, no matter how friendly or helpful he or she was.

"Can you go on by yourself?" Ebler asked anxiously. "I wouldn't want you driving with a concussion or anything."

"No, I wasn't hurt that badly. Anyway, I'm turning around and going home. I'm certainly grateful to you, Ben. I hope I can do the same for you sometime."

Ben laughed. "I hope not. I don't look forward to having a couple of gangsters jump me. Well, good night, Frank."

Frank entered the house as quietly as he could. His mother and Aunt Gertrude were watching TV in the study and he could hear them laughing. He slipped into his father's study and used the phone there to call the hospital.

"Do you have a nurse named Ted O'Neil?" he asked the woman at the desk.

"No. We have a Mary O'Neil, though."

"Thank you," said Frank and hung up. Next, he went to the laboratory above the garage. He took a cassette out of a file drawer. The Hardys always made a copy of any original tape as a precaution against theft or misplacement. Stealing the tape from Frank's pocket had done the thugs little good if their purpose was to prevent the Hardys from listening to it.

Maybe there's something I missed when I checked it out this afternoon, Frank said to himself. He put the cassette into a player and turned the volume high. Sam's mumbles became a roar, but Frank was not worried about disturbing anyone because the room was soundproof.

In his delirium Sam had said something that sounded like *sheen* over and over again. Now, with a loud volume, Frank could make out a syllable uttered before that word. "Ma-sheen, ma-sheen," droned Sam.

"Machine!" Frank repeated, snapping his fingers. "But—what kind of machine does he mean?"

He took out the tape and, picking up a portable recorder, went into their bedroom. Joe was sleeping heavily and it took several shakes to rouse him. He looked at his older brother through bleary eyes. "What is it?"

Frank told him about the attack, but added, "That's not important now. Listen, do you hear Sam say 'machine'?" He played a minute of the tape.

"It sounds like it," Joe said. "But it doesn't make any sense!"

"Nothing in this case makes any sense so far," Frank agreed.

They stared at each other in bewilderment until

76

Joe said, "I'm too tired to think. I'm going back to sleep."

There was no time to think about the tape in the morning, either. Messages concerning Bantler were piling up. The youths sifted through the heaps of telegrams and teletypes arriving from the police of various cities in the United States who had had contact with Bantler at one time or another.

By lunch, Frank and Joe decided they had learned very little about the criminal. Not even the several descriptions given by agencies who had arrested him furnished any clues. Somehow, Bantler had managed to look different each time.

"Probably the only people who can identify him are his friends and Sam Radley," Frank said.

Joe glanced at his notes. "Well, we do know he's a genius when it comes to doing anything that's mechanical. He's a whiz at handling electricity, electronics, plumbing, anything like that."

Just then the phone rang. "What have you learned?" Fenton Hardy asked from Chicago.

Frank told him of their meager results.

"Well, it's better than nothing," his father said, sighing. "We've had a little progress on this end. We've been grilling this former associate of Bantler's for hours. He said that he had met with Bantler a few weeks ago. Bantler was very excited about

77

what he termed 'a big operation, the biggest of my life.'"

"Did the associate say what it was?" Frank asked eagerly.

"No. But supposedly Bantler claimed that if things came out the way he wanted, he wouldn't have to do con jobs ever again. This associate wanted to be included, but Bantler told him he had enough henchmen. The only other thing the man was able to learn was that the operation had something to do with four-headed dragons."

"Four-headed dragons?" exclaimed Frank. "That's what the crooks mentioned when they broke into our house."

"Yes. Odd, isn't it?" said Fenton. "Well, I have to go back to the interrogation. Personally, I think we've squeezed out of this fellow all the information he has, but there's no harm in one more try. How's Sam?"

Frank told him of the operative's improvement.

"That certainly is encouraging," said his father. "I'll be in touch soon."

"You didn't tell him how those guys jumped you last night," Joe said after Frank has put down the receiver.

"He seemed to be in a hurry," Frank explained. "I'll tell him next time he calls. I've been thinking about that tape. How did those creeps know that we had taped Sam? We didn't tell anyone and we talked about it only at home."

"There's no way they could have learned about it," Joe said as they left the lab and joined Aunt Gertrude and their mother in the living room. "Yet they did. Maybe they're psychic!"

Frank laughed. "You mean they are able to know what we are thinking? That's the wildest theory you've ever come up with."

"You have a better idea?" Joe said in an offended tone.

"No," Frank conceded, "but there's got to be a more rational explanation than that."

Aunt Gertrude had a map of the eastern coast of the United States stretched out before her on the table, and pointed at it. "The hurricane is about here." She indicated a spot on the Atlantic Ocean. "And it's coming fast. The radio says it will hit this afternoon unless it veers away."

This time the other Hardys took her seriously. "We'd better prepare for it," said Mrs. Hardy. "It's good you bought those canned goods, Gertrude. Boys, you check the yard, will you, please? See that nothing is left out that might be blown away."

"Will do," said Joe. "There's the telephone again. I'll get it."

"Seems as if the whole world has been calling during the last two days," said Aunt Gertrude.

79

When Joe picked up the phone, he heard Dr. Kelly thunder from the other end of the line, "How come you contacted a New York City neurologist to come to examine Sam without even having the courtesy of informing me?"

"But we didn't," protested Joe. "We don't know anything about it."

The physician was not to be placated. "Maybe your father requested it."

"No, that couldn't be. He called us just a little while ago from Chicago and I'm sure he would have mentioned it. What did this doctor say, anyhow?"

"How do I know? He came when I was off duty."

"I don't understand," said Joe. "Did he hurt Sam?"

Doctor Kelly's voice lowered. "You really don't know anything about this, do you? There's something very wrong here, Joe. This so-called doctor took Sam away!"

10 *The Hurricane*

"Whatever happened to Sam in those woods—whatever he knows—must be very important to someone," Joe said as he and Frank drove on Main Street toward the hospital. "It sure took a lot of nerve to pose as a doctor and kidnap Sam in broad daylight."

"Was it Slicer and his friends?" wondered Frank aloud.

"I bet it was," Joe agreed and hit his palm with a fist. "I sure hope we'll catch up with Slicer again. Taking a sick man out of his bed like this is the limit!"

Dr. Kelly was waiting for them in the hospital lobby. "Our suspicions were correct," he said. "I

81

phoned the New York City hospital Morrison was supposed to have come from. They never heard of him, but one of their ambulances was stolen yesterday. Sam was taken away in that hospital's ambulance, according to one of our orderlies whom the fake doctor asked to help with the stretcher! The nerve of it, the very nerve!" The face of the usually genial doctor was a storm cloud.

"What happened to Ethel?" asked Joe. "I thought she was staying here all the time."

"Oh, she was," said Dr. Kelly bitterly, "but she received a phone call in the room just before this Morrison arrived. It was supposed to be from me, asking her to meet me at the cafeteria for lunch so we could talk over Sam's condition. She says it sounded just like me, too."

"Where is she now?" asked Frank.

"She's suffering from shock, poor woman. You can understand why. First her husband is found in a delirious state. Then he starts to recover and is snatched away. I gave her a sedative and put her to bed."

"Was Morrison alone?"

"No. The orderly said there was a driver in a white coat, a small man with scars all over his face."

"Slicer!" the Hardys said together.

"You know him?" Dr. Kelly asked, surprised.

"We've met," Frank replied. "Did you notify the police?"

"Not yet," the physician said. "What with everything happening and taking care of Mrs. Radley, I haven't had a chance."

"Never mind," Frank said. "We'll do it."

The youths used the phone at the lobby desk to call Chief Collig. "I wish Dr. Kelly had contacted me immediately," said the police officer. "We might have prevented the ambulance from leaving the city. It was found five minutes ago out of town on Route 13. No one in it, of course. They must have transferred Sam to a car. We'll send out an all-points alarm."

"What do we do now?" Joe asked as they walked out of the hospital.

Frank shrugged. "What can we do? We have no clues at the moment to follow up. We'll just have to wait to see what the police find. Remember what Dad said: waiting is tough, but sometimes it is the only thing to do."

"I hate to tell him about Sam being kidnapped with all the problems he's now facing," Joe said. "And here comes another problem—Aunt Gertrude's hurricane."

Dark clouds were rolling in from the south. A sharp wind blew over the parking lot and large drops of rain began to fall.

"I know what we should do right now," said Joe when they got into the car. "We should check the *Sleuth*."

"Good idea," said Frank, starting the engine. The *Sleuth* was their motorboat, which was moored at the Bayport Marina. As they headed toward the docks, Joe turned on the radio and they listened to a weather report. The hurricane's center was going right over Bayport, the announcer told them. Winds were going to be very high, accompanied by heavy rain. The only happy note was that the great storm would not last long since it was traveling quickly. It was expected to be out of the area sometime in the night. The name the U.S. Weather Bureau had given to the hurricane, the radio announcer added, was Gertrude.

The Hardys laughed. "Aunt Gertrude's own hurricane," said Joe.

"She'll never get over it," said Frank as they arrived at the dock. The *Sleuth* was in its berth, bouncing up and down in the rough water. One of the lines that attached it to the dock was loose and the boys secured it tightly. Then they made sure the canvas cover was fastened properly.

"Look!" Joe exclaimed suddenly, pointing out to the bay. "Someone's out there!"

Visibility was poor, but Frank narrowed his eyes and peered through the slanting rain. He was barely able to make out a person waving from a drifting boat.

"You run down to the Coast Guard," he shouted above the howling wind, "and I'll go out!"

Joe needed no second bidding. He turned on his heels and dashed for their car. Frank quickly untied the lines securing the *Sleuth* to the dock and tore off the canvas cover. In a minute, the engine was purring smoothly and the boat was heading out of the marina. "I hope I can get there in time," the boy muttered.

The Coast Guard station was half a mile from the marina. Ordinarily, it would have taken only a few minutes to get there, but a tree had fallen across the road. After climbing over it, Joe sprinted the last four hundred yards.

He burst into the building. A chief petty officer glanced up from his desk. "Boat . . . drifting. . . . Frank went after it . . ." Joe gasped.

"Catch your breath first, son," the officer said gently. "If you have an emergency, we'll be able to handle it better when we get a coherent statement."

Joe leaned on the desk for a few moments while his breath slowed. At last he was able to speak. "There's a disabled craft in the bay with someone in it. My brother Frank went out in our boat to rescue the person."

"Commander Morelli!" the officer shouted. "Boat adrift!"

From an inner office came a tall, square-faced man. Joe repeated his story. "Sound the alarm, Pete," the commander ordered the officer. "We're going out in one of the cutters."

Pete bellowed into a microphone, "All hands, hear this! Assemble on cutter three! On the double!"

There was the sound of hurried footsteps from a back room, then a group of sailors pounded through the lobby out onto the dock. In the meantime, the commander was hurriedly putting on foul-weather gear. "Come on," he said to Joe. "You can help us."

Joe ran after the commander and jumped into the cutter. Its engines were already roaring. "Cast off!" came the order and the boat moved through the rough water.

"Hope we can find your brother and the other person," said Commander Morelli grimly. This is a very powerful storm."

Frank gripped the wheel with all his might, but it was still difficult to keep the *Sleuth* on course. The boat was pushed in many directions. Once, it was even twisted back toward shore. While the young detective desperately fought to keep the *Sleuth* pointed out toward the ocean, he often lost sight of the disabled craft. Just when he thought the situation was hopeless, he caught a glimpse of the frightened person through the driving rain.

At last he was only a few yards from the drifting boat. He started to shout, but the words died on his lips as he saw a huge wave smash down on the disabled craft.

Riding up the wave and down the trough on the other side, he stared around wildly. Then he saw to his horror that the boat had overturned! A head was bobbing in the water. Frank gunned the *Sleuth* ahead and drew up beside the swimmer.

He let the wheel go and held out his arms. The stranger grabbed at his hands. Twice the slippery grip loosened and the swimmer fell back. The third time, Frank seized the other's wrists and pulled as hard as he could.

The swimmer fell head first to the bottom of the *Sleuth*, sputtering and gasping, then turned a grateful face toward her rescuer. The boy's eyes widened.

"Maquala!"

"Frank Hardy?" she stammered. "Now—now it is twice I owe my life to your family."

"I haven't saved you yet," Frank replied. "First we have to get to shore."

He turned the *Sleuth* around. Heading back to land went faster than pushing out in the direction of the wind, but it was no less dangerous. Now waves crashed from behind.

The *Sleuth's* engine suddenly coughed and died. "What's wrong?" shouted Maquala.

Frank quickly examined the motor. "I don't know, and I don't have time to fix it now."

He went back to the wheel. The boat drifted toward the faintly visible shoreline. He tried to steer in the direction of the marina, but, despite his efforts, they headed toward a rockpile east of the docks. If they hit those boulders in the heavy storm, their chances of survival would be practically non-existent!

The cutter rode slowly through the bay, horn blaring but barely heard above the screaming wind. On all sides of the Coast Guard vessel, sailors kept a keen-eyed watch.

"It doesn't look too good, son," Commander Morelli said to Joe. "We're doing our best, but you'd better be prepared for the worst."

Frank drowned? Joe could not believe it. He and his older brother had been through so much together.

"Boat drifting dead ahead!" a sailor suddenly yelled from the bow.

"Anyone aboard?" the commander shouted back.

"Two people!"

"Then prepare to come alongside her!"

Within a minute they had drawn up to the helpless *Sleuth*. A sailor threw a line down to Frank, who grabbed it and tied it to the boat. Then he helped Maquala start up a rope ladder. Joe reached out and brought her up on deck. He recovered quickly from his surprise at seeing her and grinned. "We seem to be bumping into each other everywhere."

When Frank was certain that the young woman was safe, he started up the ladder. Halfway, his foot slipped and he fell back into the churning water. He was swept away and lost from sight!

11 Amazing Rescue

Maquala, Joe, and the crew looked with horror at the roiling water, but there was no sign of Frank. Commander Morelli shook his head. "Keep your eyes peeled," he ordered his men, but it was obvious by the tone of his voice that he held little hope for the boy's rescue.

The screaming wind rocked the cutter, trying to change its direction toward the shore. "Keep it steady," Morelli told the seaman at the wheel.

Suddenly, an enormous wave reared up from seaward. Maquala and Joe gasped and seized the rail. It seemed to them that the Coast Guard craft would be crushed under the tons of water thundering down on them.

Then it hit. The youths lowered their heads to weather the shock. The water tore at them, trying to loosen their grip and would have succeeded in tossing them into the sea if it had lasted one split second longer. As it passed, there was a thud on the deck.

There was a muffled cry! The crew, Maquala, and Joe looked around and saw Frank lying on the deck, clinging to the anchor line. He was shaking and coughing violently. But soon he realized that he had been miraculously saved, and, once he calmed down, a smile of relief flooded his pale face. "Thought—I'd be done for," he sputtered.

Morelli stared at him in amazement. "I've been to sea for more than twenty years," he yelled above the storm, "and I've seen many odd things, but nothing like this! You're a very lucky person."

He and Joe helped Frank to his feet and walked him into the captain's cabin, followed by Maquala. Here the young people were wrapped in warm blankets, and the commander ordered the cutter to return to the Coast Guard station. It took half an hour for the boat to battle its way through the storm back to the dock.

Once inside the station house, one of the petty officers made some tea for Frank and Maquala. Then Morelli, who had been supervising the securing of the cutter, came in. "I hope we don't have to go out again till this hurricane is over," he said.

He turned to Maquala. "What in the world possessed you to sail out in a storm like this? You're lucky to be alive. If it hadn't been for these boys, you'd never have come back. As it was, you put the lives of my crew and Frank Hardy in great danger!"

The foreign girl lowered her head. "I am sorry," she apologized. "I did not know this storm was going to happen."

The Coast Guard officer looked at her incredulously. "Warnings were being announced over the radio all the time," he said. "You mean you never heard about it once?"

"We do not have a radio," she replied simply.

Morelli was even more astounded. "I thought all kids had radios glued to their ears continually. At least, mine do."

"I do not," Maquala said, "but if I had, I doubt I would have done any differently. I would not have known what a hurricane would be like. We do not have them where I come from."

The commander could see his scolding was not going to be effective. "Well, now you know what they're like. As none of you seem to have sustained any injuries that would land you in the hospital, you can go now. Frank and Joe, we'll keep your boat safe here until after the storm."

"Thanks, Commander," Frank said. "And double thanks for saving my life."

The seaman grinned. "All in a day's work."

"I must go home now," Maquala said as the three of them piled into the Hardys' car.

"You'll catch pneumonia before you get there," said Joe. "First come home with us so Mom and Aunt Gertrude can get you dry."

The young woman shivered. "I suppose I should. I am cold."

She continued to tremble all the way to the Hardy residence. It was a hazardous trip. Ordinarily, it took fifteen minutes to go from the docks to Elm Street. This time, three quarters of an hour passed before the boys saw the friendly lights of their house. They had had to detour several blocks because of fallen trees and telephone poles. The force of the wind was increasing and often they felt it push against them. Joe had a hard time keeping the car on the road.

Halfway up the drive, he stopped. "You two get out and run in. I'll put the car in the garage."

Maquala and Frank needed no second bidding. They jumped out and dashed through the teeming rain.

Joe moved ahead to the garage. As he approached, he pressed the button of the remote control unit and the door swung open. He drove in and had one leg out of the car when he heard the sound of running feet. Before he could react, strong hands grasped the car's door and pushed it back, pinning Joe's ankle.

Joe gasped in pain, but the pressure increased. A flashlight was snapped on and shone in his face. "Stay there real still, kid," came a rough voice. Then Joe saw the barrel of a gun.

"Slicer," he said to the man in the darkness.

"You got it right, Hardy. I've been standing out in the rain for a long time for you and your brother. It ain't no fun standing out in a hurricane. That's another one I owe you."

Despite his agony, Joe saw the humor in the situation. "I suppose that's my fault. I would have come home earlier if I knew you were here."

"You're lucky," snarled the thug. "The boss told me not to hurt you."

Joe winced in pain and looked down at his leg. "Do you think this tickles?"

Slicer snorted, but eased the door slightly. "Now listen carefully. The boss wants me to let you know that this is the last warning. Lay off!"

"Lay off from what?" Joe asked. "We don't even know what you're doing. Anyhow, you have our tape and you have Sam."

Slicer's laugh contained no humor. "Sure we have Sam, but don't give me that stuff about the tape. We know you have a copy. And don't do any more snooping if you want your friend to remain healthy. That goes for your father, too. Got that?"

Joe nodded. "I've got it."

"Last warning, remember. Now I'm going. Don't try to follow me or I may have to use this gun."

The flashlight went out and the man ran off into the rain. Joe hobbled out of the car and limped across the lawn toward the house. "Follow him?" he grumbled. "I couldn't run twenty yards!"

It was fortunate no one was in the kitchen, so he didn't have to explain the limp. He went upstairs and into the boys' bedroom. Frank was changing his clothes.

"You twist your ankle?" he asked.

"Not quite. We've had a visitor." Joe went on to relate the incident in the garage.

Frank frowned. "There's a couple of strange things about this."

"Like what?" Joe said, sitting on the bed and taking off his shoe.

"Why did he say that Dad should lay off? Slicer knows he's out of town since he tried to sabotage his plane. Apparently, he also knows that the attempt was a failure. Also, how does he know we had copied the original tape?"

Joe stopped rubbing his throbbing ankle and looked thoughtful. "I can understand how he found out Dad's plane didn't crash. If it had, he would have read about it in the newspapers or heard about it on television. But how he knew we had another tape is beyond me. It's almost as if he could hear everything that is said in this house."

"Maybe he can," said Frank grimly. "Let's look around."

They searched the room, starting with the closet. They went over every inch of the two bureaus and then the lamps. After fifteen minutes, they found what they suspected under the rug beneath Joe's bed.

Frank held up the small electronic device. "A bug!" exclaimed Joe.

"Yes," said Frank. He dropped it on the floor and crushed the tiny gadget under his heel. "There! Now those gangsters won't eavesdrop on us any more. But that's only the tip of the iceberg. I bet every room in the house has a bug."

"But how?" cried Joe. "Who could have done it?"

"Soup's on!" called Aunt Gertrude from the bottom of the stairs.

"We'd better go," Frank said. "Not a word of this to Mom or Aunt Gertrude, though."

They went downstairs where there was a hot meal waiting. "I thought stew would be just the thing for a wet day," said Aunt Gertrude.

Mrs. Hardy and Maquala entered the dining

room. "It is fortunate that Maquala and I have the same size," said the boys' mother. The girl was wearing jeans and a thick, gray sweater. "She fits into my clothes as if they had been made for her."

Outside the wind howled louder than ever, but Aunt Gertrude scoffed at the noise. "It will be all over by midnight," she announced.

"Did you hear what the hurricane is called?" Joe asked mischievously.

She sniffed. "Gertrude! Oh, yes, I heard about that, young man. I wish they would abolish this habit of naming these terrible storms after people."

"They have to be called something," Frank said.

"The first one of the year should be named 'Awful,' the second one 'Bad,' the third one 'Catastrophe,' and so on," she suggested.

The boys laughed. "Might be a good idea at that," Joe agreed.

The brothers ate ravenously, but Maquala merely picked at her food. Between infrequent bites, she raved about the boys' courage and how they had twice rescued her. Frank and Joe felt somewhat embarrassed about her praise and wished their new friend would change the subject. Aunt Gertrude and Mrs. Hardy, though, listened intently, especially to what had happened in Barmet Bay.

After a dessert of apple pie topped with vanilla ice cream, Mrs. Hardy said, "I think, Maquala, you should spend the night here. It's dangerous to drive in this weather."

The girl turned pale. "I cannot, Mrs. Hardy. My father is not a well man and he worries about me a great deal."

"You could phone him," Aunt Gertrude pointed out.

"There is no phone in the main house," Maquala said. "There is one in the cottage where the caretaker lives, but he does not like us and I fear he would not go out in this weather to carry a message to my father. I thank you for your kindness, but I really must go." She rose. "If you could show me the telephone, I will call a taxi."

"There won't be any taxis running in this storm," said Frank. "Joe and I will take you." He glanced at his mother. "Don't worry, Mom, we'll be careful."

Mrs. Hardy nodded, but her sons didn't see her whitened knuckles, hidden in her lap.

12 A Strange Visit

As before, the boys had a difficult time getting out of their neighborhood. Once on Main Street, however, the driving was easier. It was clear of obstructions and there was little traffic. Moving through the outskirts of the city, they saw that block upon block was pitch dark. "Some of these houses may be without electricity for days," Frank observed.

Joe nodded, then pointed ahead. "Look!" he cried out. They had come to a police road block. Frank lowered his window as an officer approached.

"We're trying to get people to go back to Bayport unless it is absolutely necessary for them to leave," he said. Although he was actually shouting, he could barely be heard above the screaming wind and the rain.

Frank explained their mission. "You're the Hardy brothers, aren't you?" asked the officer. "I guess Chief Collig would let you through if he were here. Okay, go ahead, but be careful. It's a mess."

Frank thanked him for the advice and went on in the heavy rain. The wipers were of little use and he could see only a few yards ahead. He drove slowly, leaning forward to keep his sight on the small strip of visible asphalt.

"You know, we're pretty lucky," Joe remarked.

Frank glanced at him quizzically. "How do you figure that?"

"Suppose this had been snow!"

"Very funny." But Frank had to grin in spite of himself. Trust his lighthearted brother to try to make the best of any situation.

Off to one side there came a sharp crack. A shadow was falling ahead of them. Frank had the impression it was a giant fist until he realized a tree had been torn from the earth. He slammed on the brakes and the car skidded a few feet before stopping a foot from the trunk.

The boys got out of the car to survey the damage. "One second more and it would have crushed us," Joe observed.

Frank shone his flashlight along the length of the trunk. "It didn't go all the way across the road. We'll be able to get around it. I just hope that other fallen trees haven't blocked the way completely."

They crawled ahead for what seemed hours, but Frank's hope was fulfilled. Although there were many trees that had crashed, they were able to skirt them. Once they passed an electrical pole pushed down by the powerful wind. The lines lay on the road, smoking and crackling with sparks of acrid-smelling electricity.

After passing the entrance to the Morton farm, they came to the small bridge. "I sure hope it stands up until we're over it," said Joe.

The twenty-foot high iron gate to the Sayer estate was closed. "If it's locked, we're going to have a hard time getting in," said Joe. He climbed out of the car and walked with difficulty against the wind to the gate. It was not locked, but he had to use all his strength to push it open. Frank drove through and Joe closed it behind them.

"Here at last!" exclaimed Joe as he jumped back into the automobile.

They inched ahead. Before them they could dimly see the enormous mansion, starkly outlined in the rain.

"Who are you?" Without warning, a figure resembling a large, flopping bird came out of the

101

bushes, holding a club. "Stop right there, I say!"

Frank almost drove off the road as he attempted to evade the stranger. The figure came up to the window and Frank saw with relief that it was a man; his oversized rain gear had only made him look birdlike.

"Get out of here!" the man screeched. "This is private property!"

"Mr. Grabb, it's me, Maquala," called the Krazak girl. "These young men have brought me home."

The face was wizened and lined. Darting eyes focused on Maquala. "Oh, it's you," came the querulous voice whose tone betrayed a dislike for the girl. Emile Grabb lowered his club. "I've been on the lookout for thieves. They've tried so often to rob Miss Sayer, but I've stopped them every time."

"You think they'd come in a hurricane?" asked Joe incredulously.

The caretaker looked at him with contempt. "What better time? They would hope to catch me off guard. Miss Sayer's orders are to be especially watchful in this kind of weather." He straightened and gestured toward the mansion. "Go on!"

"He talks as if Miss Sayer were still alive," said Frank, putting the car into low gear and moving foward.

"To him, she still is, I think," Maquala said. "Poor

man. He doesn't like any of us, but I feel sorry for him."

"I guess when you've been taking care of a hotel for ghosts for so many years," said Joe, "it's easy to believe she's still around, watching his every move."

Frank stopped the car and the three got out. As they approached, the front door was flung open and Tonio squinted out into the rainswept darkness. "Who are you? What are you doing here?" he shouted.

"Tonio! It's me, Maquala!"

The young foreigner threw an arm around the girl's shoulders and drew her inside. "Maquala, how worried we have been! We didn't know what happened to you. We called the police from the caretaker's cottage, but they knew nothing. Where have you been?"

"Oh, Tonio, I have so much to tell you." She then began speaking rapidly in a foreign language that neither Hardy recognized. It was obvious, however, that she was relating her experience in the boat, for she pointed to Frank and Joe from time to time. Tonio's frown deepened as he glanced at the brothers.

At last, Maquala stopped talking. Tonio turned toward Frank and Joe. "Thank you for what you have done," he said in a surly tone. "Thank you for saving her life."

"You did the same for me," returned Joe.

Tonio looked as if he regretted that he had trailed the wild dogs. "You go now."

"That's no way to act," Maquala cried. "They took me to their house when I was wet and shivering and their mother and aunt took good care of me. Frank and Joe certainly deserve as much from us."

Tonio was about to retort, but was cut short by a voice from the stairs. "Maquala!" A short plump man bounded down the steps and enfolded the girl in his arms. Once again, the two conversed in the foreign language. Finally, the man came toward the Hardys, a wide smile on his face. He held out his hand.

"You are a million times welcome! I am Alessandro Krazak, Maquala's uncle. I fear she has put you to some trouble and, according to her, you were exposed to a considerable amount of danger." The uncle shook both boys' hands vigorously and then beamed at them, his enormous mustache lifted by his grin. "Come, come into the living room. Tonio, fetch glasses of tea and be sure they are boiling hot."

Alessandro herded the young people through a door while Tonio disappeared in the opposite direction. The "living room" was as large as a tennis court. Faded tapestries lined the walls. The floor was covered with worn Oriental carpets. A huge log was burning and snapping in a fieldstone fireplace.

Alessandro led the Hardys and his niece to two large leather couches before the flames. He amiably spoke to them and from time to time gently scolded Maquala for going out in the boat.

Ten minutes later, Tonio entered, carrying steaming glasses of tea on a silver tray. He solemnly presented the tray to the Hardys. The glasses almost burned the brothers' hands at first and they had difficulty holding them, but a few sips made them warm and comfortable.

Tonio sat on the other couch next to Maquala and the conversation continued. Frank and Joe eventually noticed that Alessandro was plying them with questions while diverting their queries about the Krazak family and life in Eastern Europe. They realized that they were undergoing a gentle but clever interrogation.

At last the Hucul took a large swallow of tea and put the glass down. "I am sure that my brother, Maquala's father, would personally like to thank you for what you have done. However, his health is fragile. He is resting at the moment and I should not like to disturb him."

It was a form of polite dismissal and the Hardys

rose. They were about to say good-bye when a far door opened.

"Maquala, where have you been? And who are these people? You remember my rule about never allowing strangers in this house!"

Joe and Frank turned to see a small, thin man in a wheelchair glaring at them!

13 The Mysterious Wing

For the third time, the Hardys heard their exploits told in the mysterious foreign language. The crippled man's grim face never changed expression, but there was a softening in his eyes. He pulled Maquala to him and kissed her. Then he pressed a button on the wheelchair and came forward to the Hardys.

"Please excuse me if my greeting was not proper or polite," he said, "but understand that we have been under a great deal of pressure. Also, I am not the diplomat my brother is. I am Dubek Krazak and I thank you for twice saving the life of my only child. I thank you from the bottom of my heart."

"We were glad to do it, sir," said Frank.

"Good-bye, then. Tonio, come with me. I need

you." With a curt nod toward the Hardys, Dubek Krazak turned and wheeled out of the room, followed by a silent Tonio.

"I think we ought to be going now," said Joe.

"Not yet," said Maquala. "Why, you haven't even seen the house."

"They know best, my dear," said Alessandro nervously. "They have to drive back through the hurricane—"

"Oh, it will only take a few minutes," she interrupted. She looked at Frank and Joe. "Don't tell me you are not burning with curiosity," she teased. "I've heard everybody in Bayport would love to be shown through Abby Sayer's haunted house."

"I'd go through a thousand hurricanes to explore it," Joe said impetuously.

"I don't know if I would go that far!" Frank laughed. "But it's true I would like to see it."

"Then come along," she said.

Her uncle sighed. "I'll come, too."

"There once were over three hundred rooms," Maquala said as they walked through the large circular foyer and up the winding stairs, "but just before Abby Sayer died, one wing burned to the ground. There are still about two hundred rooms." She opened a door in the hall on the second floor. "Look."

The young men peered within. It contained one

white iron bed, a mahogany bureau on which stood an old-fashioned washbowl, and a cedar chest. Facing the single window were two rocking chairs.

"This is a ghost's room," Maquala explained. "Every other ghost's bedroom is the same—exactly the same, the furniture, the bed, the chest, the one window. And each room measures exactly twenty-four feet by twenty-four feet."

"There's no closet," said Joe.

She giggled. "There's none in any ghost's room. I suppose she thought they never took off their ghostly suits and dresses."

Frank didn't believe in ghosts, but he had an eerie feeling as he looked in the stark room. If I stayed here long enough, he thought, I might begin seeing things.

Next, Maquala took them up and down several staircases. "Don't you notice anything similar about the stairs?" she asked at last. They stared at her in bewilderment and shook their heads.

"They all have thirteen steps!"

"This one doesn't go anywhere," Joe said after he mounted one staircase and found himself facing a blank wall.

"Oh, there are a lot of them like that."

"Why?"

The young woman shrugged her shoulders.

"Only Abby Sayer knew. Let's go up to the clock tower. It will be exciting in this storm."

"I don't think we should," Alessandro warned. "It might be dangerous. Anyway, you certainly have had enough excitement in one day, I think."

But Maquala disregarded his objections with a laugh, and climbed a ladder to the trapdoor. The others followed her. "Do you still have your flashlight, Frank?" she asked.

"Right here."

"Good. We're in the attic and there are no lights."

Frank snapped on the flashlight and examined the attic, which seemed as large as a football field. In the center were wooden stairs leading upward.

"We have to go up there," Maquala said and ran to the steps. Alessandro again protested, but there was no stopping the headstrong girl. They climbed within a tall, dark column.

"What's that?" asked Joe as they passed a round mechanism with many large gears.

"The clock," Maquala replied, "but it does not work any more. It is said that it stopped the second the old lady died."

They emerged from the stairs onto a platform. All around them were windows and Maquala was right; the scene was exciting. Dark shadows of trees below

110

them waved bony arms at the sky. Menacing clouds whipped by overhead and the wind rattled furiously at the old windows.

"Look!" whispered Maquala, pointing toward the back of the strange building. They could vaguely see the ocean, its waves mounting high and smashing against the rocks below. "The mansion is built on the edge of a cliff," she said. "Someday it will slip into the sea, ghosts and all!"

Alessandro shuddered. "I think it might happen any minute," he said. "I can feel this tower shaking."

"I can't," his niece declared.

"I can," Frank said. "That's a powerful wind. Let's go down."

"All right," she said. "I have a number of other things to show you, anyhow."

"This sure is the best way to see a ghost hotel," Joe said as they descended. "At night, during a hurricane. It had three hundred rooms once, you say?"

"Yes, until there was a fire. You know, Abby Sayer really wasn't very friendly with her ghosts. She was afraid of them. She used to sleep in a different room every night and not even the servants knew which one she picked. They thought she was in the wing that burned during the fire, but she wasn't. It took a long time to search the remaining bedrooms. When they found her, she was sitting up in bed, petrified."

"How do you know all this?" asked Joe.

"Emile Grabb can't resist telling the story of the mansion when he is asked. I've learned a lot from him."

"You shouldn't put any stock into what that crazy old man says," Alessandro remarked.

"I don't," she replied, "but they are good stories. They help to pass the time."

The group went down to the main floor again and Maquala guided them along a long, dark hall. She pushed open a large door at the end and snapped on the light.

Before them was an immense room with a large table in the middle. There were six chairs on either side and one chair at the head.

"This is where Abby Sayer dined with twelve ghosts each midnight," Maquala said.

Joe and Frank could imagine the scene: the old woman sitting alone at the end of the table, talking to empty chairs.

Maquala switched off the light and closed the door gently. Then she took them back through the corridor. When she approached the foyer, she turned to a small door on her right. "Now you can see the wing that was left standing after the fire."

"No, no, Maquala," Alessandro said, bounding ahead to stop her. "Not that door!"

But he was too late. She was already turning the knob. Suddenly, someone opened the door from the inside and Tonio came out. He closed the door quickly behind him, but not before the Hardys had seen some men on the other side seated around a table.

Joe had recognized one of them—Slicer! A chill ran down the boy's spine, and he looked at Frank to see if his brother had made the same discovery. But Frank's face was calm and impassive.

"You must not go in, Maquala," Tonio said coldly. "Your father is working in there."

She pouted. "I'm never allowed in. You and Father and Uncle go in and spend the day, leaving me all alone to wander around the rest of the house. I don't see why I am barred."

"It's because your father loves you so very deeply," said Alessandro. "He couldn't bear to see you hurt. The work he is doing is very dangerous."

"He never tells me anything," she grumbled. "I don't even know what this invention is that he is working on. I think—"

Her complaint was cut off by a sudden pounding on the front door. "More visitors!" Tonio shouted. He stamped across the foyer toward the door with everyone right behind him.

There in the rain stood Emile Grabb, his floppy clothes making him look more like a great bird than ever. He was holding his club threateningly over a bedraggled figure at his side.

"I found this trespasser snooping around, trying to find Miss Abby's treasures, no doubt," he said in his squeaky voice. "He claims to know you, but I think he is lying."

The Hardys almost burst out laughing. The pitiful "trespasser" was none other than Chet Morton!

14 A Coded Message

"Don't hit him, Mr. Grabb!" cried Maquala in alarm. "Why, he's our next-door neighbor."

"That's the worst kind," retorted the caretaker. "Okay, sonny, you can go in, but don't try any funny business. Don't want to catch you taking any of Miss Sayer's stuff."

"Why would I want to do that?" said Chet faintly.

"Come in, come in, both of you. Now what is this about?"

No one had heard Dubek Krazak entering the foyer in his rubber-tired wheelchair.

"I'm here to deliver a message from Frank and Joe's mother," explained Chet. "I almost didn't make it because the bridge collapsed after I went over it and—"

"All right, all right," Maquala's father snapped. "What is the message?"

"Mrs. Hardy wants Frank and Joe to know that their father phoned from Chicago. He said that the informer admitted that he saw Bantler—"

Frank and Joe had been giving their friend frantic signals to stop, but Chet had been too distracted by Emile Grabb to notice. Now Joe interrupted the chubby boy firmly.

"Chet, Dad's messages are always confidential!"

Chet turned red. "Oh, I'm sorry, but—"

"You understand," Frank explained to the others, "that we're not allowed to discuss our father's cases with anyone." He stepped up and pulled Chet aside. Joe joined them.

"Now, what's this all about?" Frank asked in a low tone.

"The informer said that Bantler was going to some hideout on the East Coast for a short time, then would be heading for Alaska to destroy large sections of the oil pipeline. Your father's coming back from Chicago immediately. You've got to pick him up at the airport."

Frank and Joe stared at Chet in amazement.

"Your dad knows about the hurricane," Chet

116

went on. "It's supposed to be over in a few hours. He'll land as soon as he gets word from Bayport Airport."

"We'd better leave right away," Joe said.

"You can't. As I said before, the bridge collapsed and the only way to get back to town is to detour north about forty miles. And it would be very dangerous since a lot of trees have fallen. I can't even go home because of the bridge, and I live right next door!" Chet's voice had become loud and excited again.

The Hardys did not see the sharp glances Dubek exchanged with Tonio and Alessandro, and the hand signal he gave them. Suddenly, before Joe had a chance to tell Frank and Chet about Slicer, the scientist wheeled himself up to them.

"Since your friend reported that the bridge is down, you boys must stay here for the night, or at least until the storm passes," he said in a friendly tone. "I would never forgive myself if you left and were injured after saving my daughter's life."

"Why, thank you very much, Mr. Krazak," Frank said. "We're happy to accept your invitation."

Joe was glad his brother had gone along with Krazak. Perhaps this way they could explore the mansion!

"But we must let our mother know where we

are," Frank went on. "Otherwise she'll be worried."

Dubek Krazak held up his hands in a gesture of helplessness. "I wish we could accommodate you, but unfortunately there is no telephone in this house."

"Mr. Grabb has one, I believe," Frank said with a cool smile.

There was a glint of anger in the scientist's eyes. "I suppose it's all right, if Mr. Grabb will allow it."

The caretaker scowled and scratched his head. "Well, I don't know—" He turned to the Hardy brothers. "Fenton Hardy is your father?"

"That's right."

"I do recall that Miss Sayer thought highly of him."

"Did she know him?" Joe asked.

"Oh, not personally, but she used to read about him in the newspapers. She admired the way he solved crimes. Ought to be more people like him, she said. I guess it's okay to use my phone. Come along!"

Dubek looked at Tonio and made a small nod. The young man said, "I will go with you." He looked sourly at Joe and Frank. "Just in case you fall down and hurt yourselves."

Led by Emile Grabb, the Hardys, Chet, and Tonio trudged out into the wind and rain. It was

118

difficult keeping a sure footing on the dirt drive, which had turned to mud. Joe pretended to slip. "I can't stay up. I shouldn't have worn these jogging shoes. Frank, Chet, let me hold on to you."

He put his arm around Frank's and Chet's shoulders and then said just loud enough to be heard above the storm, but out of Tonio's earshot, "One of the men sitting in that room with Dubek was Slicer!"

"Are you sure?" asked Frank.

"Positive!"

"All the more reason for us to stick around."

At last, they reached the caretaker's cottage by the gate. Emile Grabb opened the door and pointed to the telephone on a small table. "There it is. While you're all here, could one of you help me with a crate in the cellar? I've been waiting for someone to come around and give me a hand."

Chet, who had sunk into an easy chair, made no attempt to get up.

"All right, I'll do it," Joe volunteered. He left with Grabb while Frank went to the phone. "I hope the lines are still up," the young detective said anxiously as he dialed. "Yes, they are. It's ringing."

"Thank goodness," Chet murmured.

"Hello, Aunt Gertrude?" Frank said. "How is it going over there? Yes, I know we didn't bring the garden chairs in. We didn't have time. They're blown over into the next street? We'll pick them up tomorrow.

"Look, we have Dad's message. Chet got through. But the bridge is washed out. We can't get away until the storm is over, and even then we'll have to take a long detour home. Maybe Chief Collig could pick Dad up at the airport. Yes, I said Chief Collig. Tell Mom, will you, that we'll be home as soon as possible."

During the conversation, Chet had stared at his friend curiously. Frank seemed very nervous. Had the remark about Slicer disturbed him that much? He was so keyed up that he kept tapping the phone with a pencil all the time he was talking.

"Are you finished?" Tonio asked when Frank had said good-bye to Aunt Gertrude and put down the receiver. "No one else you have to call?"

"No one else," Frank replied as Joe walked into the room. "Let's get back now."

Chet heaved himself up reluctantly.

"Good-bye, Mr. Grabb," Frank called. "Thanks for the use of the phone."

The only answer was a distant grunt.

They battled their way back to the mansion. The foyer was empty when they returned, but the bright light was enough welcome. However, they had only taken a few steps into the house when they were plunged into darkness.

"The electrical lines must have come down," said Joe, disheartened. "This is getting worse and worse!"

15 Caught!

"Don't be afraid of the dark," said Tonio in his usual nasty tone. "We are prepared for it."

They heard him moving around the foyer. Then a match was struck and a candlewick burst into flame. Tonio held the candle near his chest, giving his face an eerie glow. If this was meant to make the atmosphere more frightening, it failed. Joe and Frank were merely amused.

"Follow me," said Tonio. He led the way up the stairs and down a hall, then opened the door to a bedroom. "Good night," he said.

Frank stood in the doorway with his arms folded. Tonio lingered, apparently waiting for Frank to enter the bedroom, but the Hardy youth remained still. "Good night," he said.

Tonio scowled, turned on his heel, and disappeared into the darkness. Frank watched until he was sure the other had left. Then he took one step into the bedroom.

"I think Tonio meant to lock us in," he whispered. He held the knob in case the young man were to sneak up and slam the door. "Now, let's examine the situation, as Dad would say. Something very strange is taking place in this house. When Tonio came out of that wing we weren't allowed to see, I noticed a ring on the third finger of his right hand—a ring with the design of a four-headed dragon!"

Chet was confused. "So what?" he asked.

"Remember the break-ins at Sam's place and our house? The burglars were apparently looking for something having to do with dragons. We overheard them say so."

"At the time," Joe broke in excitedly, "it didn't make much sense, but now it seems to tie in with what's happening here. Slicer was one of the burglars. He sabotaged Dad's plane, and he's here tonight. If only we knew what he and his gang are up to!"

"Whatever it is," Frank said, "I don't think Maquala's mixed up in it."

"No," Joe agreed. "Otherwise, she would have tried to hustle us out of the house, as her uncle wished. Also, she's being kept out of the wing where her father's working."

Frank nodded. "Well, let's get going. We have to explore the house and get to the bottom of this."

Joe reached into his back pocket for his detective kit that he always carried. The small oilskin packet, no bigger than his hand, contained strong, collapsible tools. He took out a tiny flashlight with a long, piercing beam. "I'm ready," he said.

They crept along the hall, stopping at each room. While Chet stood guard outside, Joe would shine his light around until he and Frank were satisfied that the room was empty except for a bed and a bureau.

At the entrance to the fourth room, Frank seized his brother's arm. "There, over the bed!" he gasped. "Look at that mark!"

The Hardys moved across the room. Joe's light formed a circle around the small and simple drawing of an eye. In a corner were the letters SR.

The eye was the sign Mr. Hardy's operatives used to make a trail for their friends to follow. And the SR had to be the initials of the man who had drawn the symbol.

"Sam Radley!" Joe exclaimed. "He must have

been here! Somehow, he got hold of a pencil and made the sign."

"But where is he now?" Frank wondered aloud.

Before they could discuss that question, there was a crash at the door and Chet tumbled into the room. Joe swung his pencil-sized flashlight around just in time to see Tonio slamming the door shut behind their friend. He took two giant leaps, but as he grabbed the knob, a key turned. They were locked in!

Chet slowly rose from the floor. "I never heard a thing," he groaned. "And I was listening all the time for the slightest sound. All I could hear was you. That guy's like a cat. I'm sorry to let you down."

"Don't take it too hard," Frank said. "Tonio is extremely stealthy. Remember how quietly he went through the woods when we were trailing Joe and the wild dogs? He never even broke a twig. Do you think we can break the door down, Joe?"

"With a battering ram we could," his brother replied. He had been examining the thick oak door. "But I'll try the hinges." He worked on them with his small screwdriver for a few minutes, then stood back, shaking his head. "They're rusted in."

"But we have to get out of here," Chet wailed. He walked to the single window of the room and looked out. "We'll never do it this way, though. It's a long

125

drop and right into the sea. What are we going to do?"

"For the moment, nothing," Frank said. "We'll have to be patient. I think we should relax until help comes."

"Help?" repeated Chet. "How is anyone going to know we're in danger?"

"I told Aunt Gertrude to send the police."

"I listened to you," said Chet, "and I didn't hear you say anything like that."

Frank laughed. "Remember, Aunt Gertrude has been living with three detectives for a long time. She knows Morse code as well as any of us!"

Chet snapped his fingers. "The pencil!" he cried out.

"What are you two talking about?" Joe inquired.

"When Frank was speaking to your aunt, he was tapping the phone with a pencil—in Morse code!" Chet chuckled.

"Oh, good!" Joe said. "What did you tell her, Frank?"

"That we were in danger and she should tell the police."

"Good thinking!" Chet said happily. Soon, however, his expression became worried again. "But suppose they don't get here in time? Just in case you forgot, there's a hurricane out there and the bridge is washed out."

"Let's hope for the best," Frank advised. "Meanwhile, how about some sleep? We'll need to be alert later." He looked at his watch. "It's nine o'clock," he said. "I'll stand watch till eleven, then one of you can take over."

"I'll do the second watch," Chet volunteered. "If I take the last one, I'll be so hungry that I'll probably eat the furniture."

"I'd flip you to see who gets the bed," Joe said to his friend. "But it's so dark I can't see what side of the coin is up."

"Don't you think the ghost might object?" Frank teased.

"Ghost?" Chet quavered. "What's this about ghosts?"

Joe explained how Abby Sayer had run a "ghost" hotel. "So you see, this room really belongs to a ghost."

"You can have the bed," said Chet. "I'll sleep on the floor."

"Come on, Chet," said Frank. "We were only kidding. You don't believe all that nonsense, do you?"

"Oh, no," Chet said, "but I think I'll be more comfortable on the floor. Anyway, if there really *are* ghosts, it won't make much difference whether I believe in them or not."

No amount of argument would dissuade him from lying on the hard floor. It didn't seem to disturb him, though, since in a few minutes, both he and Joe were breathing heavily in a deep sleep.

Frank spent his watch thinking about the possibilities of escape if the police did not arrive in time. Suppose the three of them charged whoever opened the door, and then ran in different directions? One or two might be caught, but the other boy would be able to get help. The young detective didn't put a great deal of hope in the plan, but it was the best he could think of.

When he woke Chet at eleven, his friend leaped up in shock. "What's up? Who are you?"

"It's Frank."

"Oh." Chet put his hand to his head. "It's all true, then? We're in the Sayer house?"

"We are."

"And we're locked in a room and there's a hurricane going on?"

"Right again."

"I thought it was a dream," Chet said mournfully. "Is it my turn for a watch?"

"You're batting a thousand," said Frank.

"I'm so tired." Chet yawned loudly. "I didn't sleep a wink."

"If you didn't sleep, how could you have had a dream?" asked Frank.

Chet thought it over. "Sometimes I dream when I'm awake."

"You do that most of the time," teased Frank, lying down. "Anyhow, I'm going to sleep. You don't have to worry about the ghost, Chet. It walked through the wall, looked at you and Joe, and said, 'Excuse me, I didn't know this room was occupied.' Then it tipped its hat and flew up through the ceiling."

"Very funny," said Chet sourly. "I don't think this is the time for humor. There are weird people in this house, we're locked up, and the biggest storm in the world is going on, and you start making jokes. If you ask me, I—"

He broke off as he realized he was talking to himself. Frank was already sleeping heavily.

The next hour was a torture for Chet. He imagined he heard all kinds of noises. He had never minded facing a flesh-and-blood opponent he could see, but sitting in the dark, open to attack by ghosts, was almost too much to bear. Even though he told himself that he didn't really believe in spirits, he was still a little frightened.

When he heard the old clock in the mansion's tower begin to toll, he actually jumped off the floor. Joe and Frank awoke immediately.

"That clock hasn't worked for years, according to Maquala!" Frank exclaimed.

"Ten . . . eleven . . . twelve!" Chet counted in a trembling tone.

"And thirteen!" Joe cried as the bell struck an extra time.

"Thirteen o'clock," said Chet after a moment of silence. "A ghost midnight. They'll be going to dinner now."

The quiet was broken by the sound of a key turning in the lock. The door was flung open and the three young men confronted Dubek Krazak in his wheelchair. His cold, poker-faced expression had changed to one of concern and fear.

"You must leave here immediately!" hissed the scientist. "You are in great danger! I cannot explain now because you have not a minute to spare. Tonio—" he pointed to the young man beside his chair who was holding a candle, "will guide you. Go anywhere, but get away from this house if you value your lives!"

Dr. Krazak then backed up, turned, and disappeared into the darkness of the corridor. Tonio beckoned, and the Hardys and Chet followed him. For a fleeting moment, Frank wondered if they were being led into a trap.

Tonio took them to the top of the stairs leading down to the foyer. "I can't go any farther," he

130

whispered. "I have to protect the old man. Get out of here and bring the police as fast as you can. Good luck!" With that, he ran down the hall.

"Come on," said Frank. "Keep your light off, Joe. We don't want to get spotted." The three youths went down the stairs as silently as possible.

"I think the door is straight ahead," Joe said. They moved in that direction. "I've got it!" he whispered as his hand made contact with the door-knob.

There was a chilling chuckle behind them and three flashlights turned on simultaneously. The youths spun around. They could not make out who was holding the lights, but they could see gun barrels pointing at them. "Look who we have here," a familiar voice sneered. "Frank and Joe Hardy!"

16 The Dungeon

"Slicer, light some candles," commanded the voice. There were the sounds of movement and a match being struck. Six candles were lit and placed on tables around the circular foyer.

"Say, there's the guy who helped me with my car!" Chet said, staring at the leader.

"Ben Ebler!" gasped Joe.

Frank bit his lip. "I should have known when we found that electronic bug. Who else had the chance to place it in the house?"

"Very clever deduction," the ringleader scoffed.

"Not clever enough," Frank said ruefully. "It's only now that I realize what your real name is. You're the man who can manage to look different each time he's photographed, the man who is a genius at electronics. You're Burl Bantler!"

The other gave a small bow. "One and the same. But, as you say, it's a bit too late to discover that fact. Yes, it went off just as I had planned. We hit a few snags here and there, such as our failure with your father's plane. But, on the whole, it was a fine scenario."

"You look on what you do as a play or a movie?" asked Frank.

"That's exactly what it is," exclaimed Bantler excitedly. "A good crime is one that is designed and carried out flawlessly. Quite like a stage play, but with the addition of danger. I am both the director and lead actor."

Joe looked at Slicer and the other crook, a tall, dignified-appearing man. "Some cast!" he said.

"Let me introduce them," said Bantler. "I believe you and Slicer Bork have met on several occasions. The other is—or was—a real actor, although not too successful until he joined us. His last starring role was Dr. Morrison. Carl Harport, take a bow. The Hardys admire your talents."

"Why don't you let me at Joe a while?" Slicer asked. "I have some debts to pay."

"You know my rules," said Bantler sharply. "No violence unless absolutely necessary."

Slicer took a step back and said in a softer voice,

"Whatever you say, Burl." He seemed afraid of the leader.

Bantler turned to the three youths. "Of course, I didn't expect this hurricane," he continued smoothly. "If it hadn't come up, we would have been on our way to Alaska an hour ago. I fear your father's perfect record of solving crimes is coming to an end, Hardys. You did get too close for comfort at times, but there is no way we can now be stopped from destroying the pipeline."

"Burl, this is all very interesting, but I think we ought to be looking for the others," said Harport nervously.

Bantler's eyes flashed with momentary anger at being contradicted, but he calmed himself quickly. "He is right," he told his prisoners. "Alessandro Krazak somehow got the clock working and it tolled several times, as you are no doubt aware. The fool probably thought that someone would notice and send for the police, but who could hear it in such weather? He is still somewhere at large in this house, as are Tonio and Dubek. I would enjoy chatting with you further, but I'm afraid catching them is a more pressing matter. Slicer, show our guests to the dungeon."

Slicer prodded the boys with his gun. "Get going!" They were pushed through a kitchen and down a long corridor, which ended at a door.

"Open it!" the man commanded. Joe obeyed and the three descended a steep staircase into a tunnel.

As they marched along, they could see by Slicer's flashlight that the walls were solid, thick rock. It was damp and moisture covered the stone.

"Here we are. You three stand with your backs to me and your hands high. No funny tricks!"

Slicer unlocked a huge door. "Hey, Radley," he yelled inside, "got some company for you. Three of your friends have come calling."

For some reason, the thug thought that was very amusing and went into peals of laughter as he roughly shoved the young men into the dark. The door slammed, was locked, and they heard him walk away, still laughing.

"Who's that?" came Sam's voice from a corner.

"Sam!" cried Joe. "It's me, Joe! Frank and Chet Morton are here, too!"

"Wait till I light a candle. That Slicer only gave us one and it's pretty small so we don't keep it lit all the time." There was a spark and then a flame flickered. Sam, holding the candle, slowly rose from a pile of hay. He stretched his aching muscles. "Reminds me of when I was in the army and we went out on maneuvers." He grinned at them. "Am I glad to see you!"

"And we're glad we found you!" said Joe. "Are you all right?"

135

"I guess so. I woke up in an ambulance and I thought I was on my way to the hospital. Instead, I was pushed into a car and brought here. I'm fuzzy about what happened since I saw that machine in the woods. But I feel okay. By the way, we've got a cellmate. Curt, wake up. We've got visitors."

A second person arose from another corner and came forward. "Is that Joe Hardy I hear?"

"Curt Gutman!" exclaimed Frank as the man shuffled into the light.

"Frank! Chet Morton! I hope you've come to take us out of here. I'm sorry that I didn't show up to lay the new carpeting, but as you can see, these guys kidnapped me when I was on my way to work and—"

"Don't worry," Frank said dryly. "You had a real expert as a replacement."

"Boys, bring me up to date, will you?" Sam requested. "What's been going on?"

"We'd better sit down," Frank advised. "This will take a while."

The five of them sat around the candle and Frank narrated the events of the past few days. "So you see, Sam, how it's all beginning to hang together now. But just how Bantler is going to destroy the pipeline is beyond us."

"I can fill you in on that," Sam said. "I saw it in

action." He shuddered. "The fact is that I was its first victim!"

"What!" Frank exclaimed.

"It all began by accident. A few days ago, I was driving through Bayport when I spotted Burl Bantler. He passed me in a pickup truck, going in the opposite direction. I managed to turn and follow him to the Sayer estate.

"He went in, but of course I didn't dare pursue him beyond the gate. I hid my car in the woods and set up a stakeout from behind bushes opposite the entrance."

"I wish we'd known!" Joe said.

"So do I. But I wasn't able to phone you or notify the police. After a few hours, I saw Bantler, Slicer, and a third man I later learned was Carl Harport. There were also two others, a man in a wheelchair and a younger guy."

Joe broke in. "The man in the wheelchair is Dubek Krazak, a scientist from Eastern Europe. The younger man is Tonio Mossesky, also a foreigner."

Sam nodded and continued. "They went into the woods on the mansion side of the road. I followed them. Tonio was carrying some kind of machine, similar in appearance to a hand-held TV camera. They walked about a mile or so when they came to

137

an old shack in a clearing by a stream. They stopped on the south side of the clearing and I hid behind a tree on the north side.

"The scientist—what is his name?"

"Dubek Krazak," Joe said.

"Right. He held the machine, pointed it toward the shack, and then I heard this whirring sound. I tell you, I've never seen anything like it. That building just melted away. It crumbled to a pile of sawdust before my eyes!"

"We saw the residue!" Chet cried out. "My father noticed it and couldn't figure out what happened."

"I tried to get away to call the police," Sam went on. "I would have made it, too, but I hadn't gone more than a few steps when a pack of wild dogs came out of nowhere and charged at me!"

"We ran into them, too," Frank pointed out. "They almost got Joe."

Sam shook his head. "Anyway, I was forced to retreat into the clearing and was spotted immediately. I heard Bantler yell, 'Give me the Annihilator,' and I saw him grab it from Krazak. Then he pointed it right at me and turned it on!"

The boys gasped.

"I have never felt such pain before," Sam went on, "and I've been through some very torturous experiences, believe me. It was as if I had been shot by a million sharp pins. My whole body was in agony. Maybe I would have dissolved like the shack if this Krazak hadn't run his wheelchair right into Bantler and knocked him over. He was yelling, 'No, no, it's not for killing!'

"The pain stopped, but I was dazed. Everything around me was in a kind of haze. I started to run . . . and that's all I remember until I woke up in that ambulance with Harcourt leaning over me. As you said, I must have wandered onto the Morton farm."

Everyone was silent for a few moments as they thought over the strange events of the past few days and their perilous predicament.

At last Frank sighed. "Somehow, we've got to find a way out of here and stop Bantler. He's going to take off for Alaska as soon as the hurricane is over."

Joe looked out of the window. "It looks like the storm is losing its force," he said gloomily. "I never thought that I would hate to see a hurricane end."

"I tried to think of how to escape," Sam said, "but I wasn't able to come up with a practical plan. Curt and I couldn't rush Slicer when he came in with food, for he always held his gun on us."

"With more of us here now, though," Joe said, "we might be able to jump him."

"From what you tell me, I doubt whether he'll return," Sam said. "Why should he? They'll leave and throw away the key!"

139

"Maybe the police will get here soon," said Chet brightly. "Also, it looks like the Krazaks are on our side now. Maybe they'll set us free."

That hope was immediately dashed. The door was suddenly opened and the two Krazak brothers and Tonio and Maquala were thrust in. The door slammed shut and the newcomers stared around them with helpless expressions.

17 An Evil Plan

"There goes that hope," Chet said gloomily.

"Oh, cheer up," Joe advised. "We've been in worse spots before." But he didn't sound convincing, even to himself.

After a quick evaluation of their predicament, Alessandro sighed. "I'm afraid I must agree with your friend, Joe. Apparently no one heard my feeble attempt for rescue by ringing the clock. In a short while, Bantler and his men will be off to Alaska while we languish here. It may be many days before we are discovered."

"By that time, we'll have starved to death," Maquala cried.

"I am deeply sorry that my invention has brought

141

all of us such peril," Dubek said in a heavy tone.

"Tell us about the four-headed dragon," Frank suggested.

Alessandro looked startled. "You know about that?"

"We don't really know what it is," Joe said.

"It's better that you don't know," Tonio declared.

Dubek waved a hand at the young man. "What difference does it make now? Anyway, they are entitled to learn what has put them in such great danger. The Four-Headed Dragon is the name of a secret organization behind the Iron Curtain. It is dedicated to overthrowing all forms of tyranny and freeing the enslaved people of Eastern Europe. Once the enemy was the Nazis. Today it is other oppressive governments."

"But what has that to do with Bantler and his gang?" Joe asked, puzzled.

"It will be simpler if we start at the beginning," said Maquala. "My father is the head of the Four-Headed Dragon. When we were forced to leave our homeland, he came to the United States to raise money for our cause. He believed that Americans, who love freedom more than any other people in the world, would be willing to donate funds."

"But he didn't want charity," said Alessandro, "so he decided to give something in return—a machine we called the Annihilator."

Now it was Frank's turn to be puzzled. "And you sold it to Burl Bantler to destroy the Alaskan pipeline?"

Dubek Krazak sighed. "Unfortunately, that has been the result, but we never intended it that way. It was not to be used as a weapon, but as a tool for industrial demolition or in place of dynamite in road construction."

He turned to Sam. "You must believe me," he said urgently. "We never meant to hurt you."

Sam grinned. "Don't apologize. You saved my life."

"You see," the scientist went on, "Burl Bantler is of Hucul parentage. He's a distant cousin of my father. For that reason, I looked him up when we came to this country. He told me he would be glad to help our cause and I trusted him. I did not know about his criminal background, so I told him of my plans to build the Annihilator. He offered to aid me with my experiments and I must admit he was a brilliant assistant."

"That figures," Frank said grimly. "He's known to the police as an electronics genius."

"We found out from bitter experience," Joe added, telling of how well the electronic bug had been placed and how the master criminal had broken through the installed burglar-proof system at the Hardy house.

"We took the Annihilator out into the woods for our first real test," Dubek went on. "It was then that I discovered how vicious Burl was when he tried to kill Sam Radley. After you had escaped, Mr. Radley, Burl revealed his true intention of using my invention, namely, to smash the Alaskan pipeline."

"Could he really do that?" asked Joe.

"Oh, yes, quite easily. You see, the Annihilator is based on high-frequency sound. You have probably heard that an opera singer can break a thin glass with her voice and that a group of marchers stepping in unison can bring a bridge down. That is roughly the principle behind the Annihilator. It emits a sound so high that not even a dog can hear it."

"And there was no way you could stop him?" Joe inquired.

"He threatened us," Tonio explained. "He said he would harm Maquala if we attempted to alert the police." It was quite evident from the young man's expression that the thought of Maquala being hurt was unbearable. "I apologize for the unfriendly way I've been acting, but I thought I could drive you away."

"You never told me," Maquala cried resentfully. "I was not even allowed to learn about the experiments."

"Don't blame Tonio, my dear," said Dubek. "I

made the decision to keep you out of this. Perhaps that was wrong, but I did not want to frighten you." He turned back to the Hardys and Sam Radley. "Bantler went crazy with rage when Mr. Radley escaped. He does not like to fail and has a fierce and almost uncontrollable temper. He was afraid that Fenton Hardy was on his trail. Why else, he reasoned, was Hardy's assistant following him?"

"That's why he broke into our house and Sam's apartment, and later took Curt's place as carpet layer," Frank said. "And that's why he tried to sabotage my father's plane and steal the tape."

Dubek nodded. "It is also why he had Sam Radley kidnapped. Even though he found nothing that showed you were on to him, he felt insecure. He was desperately afraid Mr. Radley would regain his memory and identify him."

"If only I could have remembered while I was still in the hospital!" Sam said wistfully.

"You may have noticed that I was quite cold and a bit impolite when I met you," Dubek went on. "That was done deliberately. I had hoped my inhospitable attitude would drive you away, for I feared for your lives. At that time, Burl was unaware of your presence here since he was in another wing of the mansion. When your friend, Mr. Morton, appeared and informed us that the bridge had collapsed, though, it was evident that you had to remain here. I had hoped to keep Burl oblivious of the fact that you were on the premises. However, when you and Tonio returned to the house after your phone call, Slicer saw you coming through the foyer. Later I had Tonio lock you in when you prowled around the house. I wanted to prevent you from meeting my dear cousin," he said bitterly. "But it was useless. He knew where you were all the time."

"Maybe the police will manage to get here soon," said Joe hopefully. He told the new prisoners about how Frank had transmitted a message to Aunt Gertrude.

Chet shrugged his shoulders. "They won't make it soon, I guarantee you. There's no chance of them crossing over the stream, now that the bridge is gone. That water's going a mile a minute."

"But Bantler is planning to take off as soon as the hurricane dies down," Joe cried. "If he can get out, why can't the police get in?"

"Yes, just how does he figure on leaving?" Curt asked. "He can't go toward Bayport, and the other roads will be in terrible condition. I don't see him going by boat, since the ocean will be rough long after the storm is over."

"He never misses a trick," said Alessandro. "He has a helicopter hidden under canvas on the western side of the house. I even doubt if Emile Grabb knows it's there. I overheard Slicer say that they plan to fly to a small airport in New Hampshire. There they will switch to a larger plane that will take them to Alaska."

"And we're the only people near enough to stop them!" Sam said. He struck his palm with a fist in frustration. "If only we could escape!"

For the past few minutes, Frank had been walking around the room. He turned to the others suddenly. "I think we can," he said.

18 Daring Tonio

Frank opened the one window in the room and banged against the bars on the outside. "Just as I thought. These are loose."

Sam shook his head. "Forget it, Frank. Curt and I already tried to pull them out."

"But there are more people now," the young detective declared. "More arms to pull with."

"Then what? We're on the ocean side of the house," Chet said. "Even if we manage to get those bars out, it's a sheer drop into the water."

"But I see a ledge out there," Frank said. "That may lead to another room. If someone could move along the ledge, get through the window, and slip into the hall, he could let us out!"

"Sounds crazy to me," Chet grumbled, "but I guess it's worth a try."

Joe, Frank, Sam, Tonio, and Chet gathered around the open window and seized the bars. For three minutes, they strained all their muscles. Their faces turned red, but the bars only gave an inch or two.

Then Alessandro strode up and pushed his way through to the window. "Once during World War Two, I traveled with a circus from enemy camp to enemy camp as a spy. I learned a great deal, most particularly how to be a strong man. It was, as the U.S. Intelligence services would say, a 'good cover.' "

He seized the bars, took a very deep breath and held it, then pulled. Slowly, the bars came away from the window!

The others looked at him with admiration. "That is really something!" Chet breathed.

"Yes, there is a ledge here," said Alessandro, sticking his head out into the storm. "But it is narrow and does not look strong. Whoever is going to walk on it must be light and sure-footed." He looked regretful that he could not fill this description.

· "It's up to me," said Joe. "I'm the lightest."

He started toward the window, but Tonio held out a restraining arm. "No, my friend, I must be the

149

one," he said in a far more genial tone than he had ever used before when talking to the Hardys. "You are lighter than I am, but I am more used to narrow places."

"He's right, Joe," Dubek said. "I love Tonio like a son and hate to see him taking chances, but he is probably the best qualified."

Joe nodded and stepped aside. Tonio nimbly jumped to the sill, holding both sides of the window. He stuck his head out, then turned back to the others. "I see a window forty feet or so to my left," he reported. "I'll try for that."

Cautiously, he went out on the ledge, his face to the wall of the building. He had only gone a few feet when Joe, who was looking out after him, yelled, "The ledge is crumbling!"

The wood had rotted after years of storms and winds. It cracked apart and Tonio began to fall toward the angry ocean. Joe lunged and grabbed the boy's wrist, but was yanked ahead himself. Just when it seemed that both young men would plunge to their deaths, Alessandro seized Joe's waist and pulled them back.

In a moment, Joe and Tonio were in the room again. Alessandro wiped his brow. "I'm not as strong as I used to be. That was tiring."

"Strong enough for me," Joe cried.

"Thank you," Tonio said, pumping the Hardy boy's hand.

"And now we're right back where we started," said Chet.

"Not quite," Frank said. "There's another alternative." He held up an old, rusty can he had discovered in a corner. "Kerosene!"

"What could we possibly do with that?" Maquala asked.

"Burn down the wooden door, of course," Dubek cried out. "That's what you have in mind, am I right?"

"Yes," Frank answered. "The door is fairly solid, but it is old and dry. It's worth a try. Please listen carefully, everyone. When the fire starts, lie down with your noses to the floor. If the room fills with smoke, you will find that there will be about an inch of fresh air on the floor."

Frank and Sam poured the kerosene until there was a pool by the door while Tonio helped Dubek out of his wheelchair. Sam touched the fluid with the candle. There was a *shoosh* and flames shot up. Smoke swirled above the prone bodies of the prisoners. The door caught fire and the old wood crackled.

It did not last long, though. The fire died, leaving the door charred, but still solid.

"Now what?" Chet groaned.

151

Just then, they heard a key in the lock. The door opened and Emile Grabb stood in the entrance, shining a flashlight and peering down through the smoke at the prisoners.

"What's going on here?" he shouted. "What are you doing?"

As the smoke poured out of the window, Frank jumped up. "Are we glad to see you!"

The startled caretaker drew back, holding his club high in a defensive gesture. "What are you doing to Miss Sayer's house? All these strange goings-on! First, the clock goes off. I came over and saw three men packing and making a mess of everything. They tried to capture me, but I ran away. Then I smelled smoke and found out you're trying to burn down the place!" As he spoke, his anger grew and his voice became louder. "I won't allow it! Miss Sayer was very kind to me when I was an orphan and she left the house in my care. I won't let anyone harm it!"

"We agree with you," said Frank quickly, "and we'll make it up to you. But there is no time to explain now. Those men you saw are criminals. They locked us up here and are going to escape with a weapon that will harm our country. They must be stopped and there's no time to lose!"

The smoke was slowly clearing and Emile Grabb squinted at the young detective. "You're one of the

Hardy sons, the family Miss Sayer admired. All right. I'll just have to trust you. Come along and we'll try to stop those men."

He turned and ran down the hall toward the stairs leading up to the main floor. The Hardys, Chet, Tonio, and Sam followed him to the door of the wing where the experiments had been conducted.

"Locked!" exclaimed Grabb, trying the knob. "And I left most of my keys back in the cottage." He pounded on the door. "Open up in there!"

"They won't pay any attention," Frank said.

The elderly man snapped his fingers. "I almost forgot. This isn't the only way to get into that wing."

He led the way back to the basement and past the room that had served as their prison. Alessandro was just coming out, pushing Dubek in the wheel-chair. "Where are you going?" he shouted.

"Mr. Grabb is showing us another way to the eastern wing," Tonio replied.

"Alessandro, Maquala, and I will go up to the foyer and wait for the police," Dubek said.

At the end of the corridor was a ladder nailed to the wall. Grabb flashed his light upward to a trapdoor. "Come on," he snapped, starting to climb.

They emerged into a "ghost" bedroom, from where they heard the sounds of hurried footsteps in the hall. Frank dashed out just in time to see the crooks run by. Slicer pushed the boy back as he rushed past. Frank fell against Joe and Tonio, who were right behind him. All three lost their balance and tumbled to the floor. By the time they regained their feet and ran into the hallway again, they heard a door being slammed and a lock being turned.

Emile pointed his flashlight in the direction of the sounds. It shone upon another closed door.

Tonio felt defeated. "They'll reach their helicopter in a few moments," he said. "Looks like we've lost them for good!"

19 Helicopter Chase

"You give up mighty fast," Emile Grabb growled. "If we're quick, we can still catch them."

Once again, he led the small troop up the stairs to the huge attic. They peered through a window at the western end of the room. The rain had stopped, although the wind was still high. A pale full moon whisked in and out of the fleeing clouds.

A moment later, Bantler and his men emerged from the house carrying a large bag. They hurried toward a covered object at the edge of a grove of trees.

"It's too far from the ground to jump," Tonio said. "We're no better off than before."

Emile Grabb glanced at him as he reached

underneath the window frame and picked up a rope ladder. "This is for fires," he explained. "We can go down it and surprise them." He fell silent for a moment before adding regretfully, "Only it's going to have to be you to catch 'em. I've got a bum leg." He glanced at Chet. "You'll never get through that window, either. Too fat!" Then he looked at Sam. "Nor you, fellow. You don't look too strong at the moment."

Frank and Joe tossed the rope ladder outside and saw the end hit the ground. Joe slipped out the window first, followed by Frank, with Tonio bringing up the rear. The younger Hardy noted that Bantler and his henchmen were too engrossed in pulling the canvas off the helicopter to see the descent of the three youths. We've got you now! he thought to himself.

He hit the ground softly and waited for Frank, who arrived a moment later. The rope was old, however, and its worn strands broke as Tonio was halfway down.

The young man landed catlike and unhurt, but the sound of his fall diverted the crooks' attention. Carl Harport shouted, "It's the Hardys!"

The three crooks' surprise immobilized them for a few seconds. Then they sprang into action, charging their pursuers.

Slicer was the first to reach the youths, but Joe

was ready for him. Timing his blow perfectly, he buried his fist into the gangster's solar plexus, doubling his attacker up. As Slicer bent, hands clutching his stomach, Joe seized an arm and sent the man flying through the air. Slicer landed heavily several feet away and, Joe noted with satisfaction, remained motionless.

But as Joe turned away from his opponent, Bantler's blackjack crashed down upon his head.

The boy fell, half dazed. Bantler and Harport ran at the two remaining boys, swinging their weapons. Tonio and Frank fought bravely, but soon suffered Joe's fate.

Harport was prepared to hit Frank again as the hapless youth lay on the ground, but was stopped by Bantler's words. "Leave him alone. We've got no time."

"Let me clip him a little," the ex-actor begged. "He and his brother have been such pests to us."

Bantler struck down his crony's blackjack arm. "Revenge is for fools," he snarled. "We have more important things to take care of. Help me lift Slicer and carry him to the chopper. Come on, move!"

They dragged their unconscious companion to the helicopter and unceremoniously threw him inside. Then they picked up the bag containing the Annihilator and placed it next to Slicer.

Bantler turned as he was about to enter the craft

and waved at the dazed youths still lying on the ground. "So long, Hardys. It's been a pleasure to meet you. Best regards to your father." He shut the door and the helicopter's engine began to roar. A few moments later, the craft lifted into the air. Tonio and the Hardys watched it disappear to the north.

Slowly they rose, their heads still spinning from the blows they had received. "You all right?" Sam called from the attic window.

"Yes, but they got away," Joe replied.

"I saw that," Sam shouted, "but maybe they can be cut off between here and Alaska."

The youths looked at one another. They had little hope that the police would be able to catch the elusive and clever Bantler before he destroyed the oil pipeline.

"Poor Dubek," said Tonio. "All he wanted to do was to make a peaceful and valuable invention for your country so he could help the Four-Headed Dragon organization. Now all he has accomplished has been to hurt the free world. He'll be crushed by this." He shook his head.

The Hardys could think of nothing to say to relieve Tonio's gloomy feelings. Silently, the trio started around the house toward the front door.

Suddenly, there was a roar from above. High-beam spotlights floated over the grounds of the

Sayer estate. For a moment, Frank thought that Bantler had returned. Then he caught sight of three hovering helicopters bearing the red and blue stripes identifying them as police craft.

"What do you know!" Joe shouted. "Maybe we still have a chance!"

They waved frantically, chasing the spots of lights on the ground until they were caught in one. A pilot noticed them and the choppers descended.

Emile Grabb and the others had reached the west lawn by the time Bayport and state police poured out of the helicopters, led by Chief Collig. They were followed by two familiar men.

"Dad and Jack Wayne!" Joe shouted.

Fenton Hardy jumped from the craft. "Frank! Joe! Are you all right?"

"A little dizzy from being knocked on the head," Frank admitted ruefully, "but we'll get over that."

"Aunt Gertrude said you told her something strange was taking place here. Why, there's Sam!" The detective strode ahead and grasped his assistant's shoulders. "How are you? I heard you were kidnapped. What's going on, anyhow?"

"Plenty, but there's little time to tell you the whole story now," Sam said grimly.

"He's right, Dad," said Joe. "Bantler and his gang are getting away and—"

"Bantler?" Mr. Hardy repeated, amazed.

"They have the weapon that can destroy the Alaskan pipeline," Frank broke in. "They took off in a helicopter not more than five minutes ago."

"That's quite a lead, but maybe we can catch up!" Jack Wayne exclaimed.

"Right!" Fenton Hardy agreed. "Frank and Joe, you can tell me the story on the way. Come on!"

Chief Collig, who was questioning Emile Grabb, turned around as the Hardys, Sam, and Jack started back toward one of the helicopters. "Where are you going?" he asked.

"To catch one of the cleverest crooks in the world!" Mr. Hardy shouted.

"Okay. You have my permission to fly one of our choppers!" Collig yelled back.

When they were high in the air, Mr. Hardy relaxed a little. "Now tell me exactly what has been happening," he said to his sons.

First, Sam related how he had been injured by the Annihilator, and subsequently kidnapped and brought to the Sayer mansion. Then Frank and Joe told what had happened since the last time they had spoken to their father.

When they were finished, Fenton Hardy whistled. "To think that I have been looking for a man who was working almost in my own backyard and who actually broke into my house!"

"Helicopter ahead about a mile," Jack Wayne

160

suddenly announced, "at ten o'clock." He pointed slightly to his left.

The moonlight etched the other craft against the night sky as clearly as though it was the middle of the day. Jack's passengers leaned forward anxiously.

"That's Bantler and his gang!" Joe cried.

20 Easy Target

The police craft steadily gained on the other helicopter. Bantler, apparently unaware that he was being chased, was not flying at top speed.

"He's smart," Jack Wayne said. "He doesn't want to catch up to the hurricane . . . and that's to our advantage."

It was not until the Hardys were flying beside the gangsters that the master crook noticed them. He then urged his pilot, Carl Harport, to greater speed by pounding his henchman on the back roughly and pointing ahead.

However, the police craft was a far more powerful machine and the thugs could not escape. Bantler was infuriated and shook his fist in frustration.

Harport tried several maneuvers to get away—sliding off toward the east, flying higher, flying so low as to almost touch treetops—but Jack Wayne kept up with him.

"He hasn't a chance," said Fenton Hardy's pilot triumphantly. "I think we ought to call in at this point."

He radioed Bayport's police headquarters and gave his position and the direction in which they were flying. "Please contact police units and military installations ahead," he asked. "Request them to send up interceptor craft. If we get enough in the air, we can force Bantler down."

"Never!" Bantler broke in. He had monitored the transmission and his voice crackled with anger and hatred. "I'm not going to let you guys stop me when I'm so near. Get away! Get away, I tell you, or you'll regret it!"

"Be realistic," Fenton Hardy replied coldly. "Don't do something you'll regret."

Bantler's answer was a curse, then he turned off his radio. They saw him shake Slicer, who had been holding his face in his hands, still recovering from his fight with Joe, into full consciousness. The two then struggled to open the large bag between them and took out a heavy machine.

"They're going to use the Annihilator on us!" Sam breathed, shuddering as he recalled his encounter

163

with Dubek Krazak's invention. "If it hits us, this copter will crumble into dust!"

In horror, the Hardys, Jack, and Sam watched Slicer balance the Annihilator on Bantler's shoulder. Once again the gang leader's voice sounded over the radio.

"We'll blast you out of the sky as we will do to anyone who is in our way!" With that, Bantler aimed the machine at them.

Jack Wayne swooped downward out of the way. He straightened out about a hundred feet below. Bantler's desperate voice screamed at them over the radio once more. "That won't do you any good! We'll hit you sooner or later!"

Harport brought his craft down to the same level as the Hardy helicopter. Once more the Annihilator was aimed. Once more Jack Wayne skillfully escaped, this time climbing above the attacker.

Harport jerked his controls and the Bantler copter listed to a forty-five degree slant. Then . . .

"Something's wrong!" yelled Joe. "They're going down!"

Harport frantically tried to straighten out, but it was too late. Down, down, down spun the criminals' machine. The Hardys, Jack Wayne, and Sam gazed at the plummeting craft in horrified fascination.

The helicopter smashed into a lake, but the

criminals managed to jump out just before it struck the water. Fenton tapped Jack on the shoulder. "Down," he ordered.

The pilot descended and a moment later they landed gently some distance from the lake's shore. In the moonlight, they saw Harport and Slicer swimming toward the beach.

Then the criminals changed direction. But they obviously did not have the strength to strike out for the opposite side, so they started for a spot about a hundred yards from the Hardy party.

Fenton Hardy pulled two pairs of handcuffs from his pocket and handed one to Sam. "Let's go!" The detective and his assistant hurried toward the gangsters' destination, followed by Jack and the boys.

"Where's Burl Bantler?" Joe cried suddenly.

"Guess he went down with the craft," Jack replied.

"No, there he is," said Frank, pointing toward a struggling figure in the middle of the lake. "Either he doesn't know how to swim or he's got a cramp."

The youths sprang into action. Peeling off their jackets and shoes, they dove into the water. They swam as fast as they could, keeping their eyes on the desperate Bantler. They reached him just as he was sinking, grabbed him, and began the torturous return trip.

When they arrived, Sam and Fenton were waiting with their captives. Fenton slipped handcuffs on the man who had eluded him so long and then put a coat over his shivering body.

Before they got into the helicopter, Bantler looked at Frank and Joe curiously. "Here I tried to kill you and yet you risked your lives to save me. Why?"

Joe grinned. "Well, Mom and Aunt Gertrude said you did a fine job on the new carpets and we thought you deserved something for that."

The three criminals were taken to the Bayport jail, then Mr. Hardy and his companions returned to the Sayer mansion.

"That is the end of the Annihilator," Dubek Krazak said when he heard his invention was at the bottom of the lake.

"Why?" Fenton Hardy asked. "You can build another one, or we might recover this one by dragging the lake."

The scientist smiled wanly. "Why do that? It has only brought evil. It has proved to be an instrument of death and destruction!"

"But it can be an instrument for good," Fenton replied. "Look at dynamite. It can kill people, but it is also essential in so many worthwhile activities."

"You argue well," said Alessandro, "but we

couldn't rebuild it, anyhow. We have very little money left."

"Don't worry about that," said the detective. "I have plenty of friends who would be eager to invest money to help you."

Tonio and Maquala had been standing together silently, holding hands. Now they came forward to Joe and Frank.

"Tonio has something to say," said Maquala.

The young man looked embarrassed as he struggled to get the words out. "I—we have a lot to thank you for. If it hadn't been for you—" he waved a hand helplessly, "well, I just want to thank you for all you have done and I deeply apologize for the way I have treated you."

Now it was the Hardy youths' turn to be embarrassed. Fortunately, they were saved by Emile Grabb who was looking with dismay at the huge house. "I will never rent the mansion again."

Fenton knitted his brow. "You talk as if it is your decision. I don't understand—"

"I own it!" exclaimed the caretaker irritably. "Abby Sayer left it to me, but only her lawyers know that. I've tried to keep the building in good condition because I promised her on her deathbed I would do so. But the cost of maintenance has been too much for me in the last few years. That's why I told the lawyers to rent it. But no more, never again! Better it should become a ruin!"

"I can see your point, but I have an idea," said Fenton Hardy. "Why not turn the mansion into a museum? People have always been curious about the house. I think they would come from near and far to take a tour of it. You could be their guide and the admission prices would be more than enough to maintain the building."

Grabb snapped his fingers. "That's great! Now I can see why Miss Sayer had such respect for your brains. I'll do it."

The gray streaks of morning began to stretch across the sky. Frank stared thoughtfully into the distance. What would the next day bring? Would there be another challenge for the Hardy boys? He had no idea that soon they would be called upon to solve a strange case called *The Infinity Clue*.